BEYOND
THE
BRIDGE

Also by Jack Matthews

HANGER STOUT, AWAKE!

BITTER KNOWLEDGE

AN ALMANAC FOR TWILIGHT

JACK MATTHEWS
BEYOND THE BRIDGE

HARCOURT, BRACE
& WORLD, INC.
NEW YORK

For Barbara,
as always . . . and for
Za, Barbie, Johnny,
Mother, Bea,
and J. C. . . . and in memory
of my father.

In the following narrative I have referred to the Silver Bridge, crossing the Ohio River at Point Pleasant, West Virginia, which collapsed on December 15, 1967. I have used the actual date of the event, the actual dimensions of the bridge, and have paraphrased a few newspaper accounts of eyewitnesses' impressions of the tragedy. Beyond this, however, I have not gone. I have not heard of, read of, or acquired anything in the way of surmise or information that the condition of my protagonist resembles that of any real person, living or dead. To the best of my knowledge, I do not know anyone who was connected in any way with the Silver Bridge collapse, nor have I heard any accounts whatsoever—firsthand or otherwise—recording information of firsthand impressions of that event. My information about the tragedy was gotten entirely from newspaper stories at the time of the tragedy. In short, the characters, along with their names and personal conditions in which they find themselves, are all totally invented. Any resemblance between them and real persons, living or dead, is completely coincidental.

BEYOND
THE
BRIDGE

I am alone in my room. The room is small, and smells of stale sunlight. And the only furniture is the cot I sleep on, a cheap, yellow plywood dresser, an old rocker with burst springs, and a straight-backed chair.

There are no curtains in the room's only window, but there is a dark green blind that has a cracked and torn edge, which someone has tried to fix with Scotch tape. Beyond the window, there is a street between dusty old buildings. This is a small town in West Virginia, hardly more than a cluster of buildings, and the people here are virtually all poor and ignorant. The town itself is shabby and dirty. All around it there are cool green mountains rising drunkenly steep and exalted into the air—emphasizing the sordidness of man by their clean aloofness.

I am sitting on the bed as I write. The big lined pad that will become my diary is on my lap, and I am etching these words with a yellow pencil. It is so hot and humid my shirt and pants are soaked with perspiration, and the dark blind rattles now and then as hot air blows into the room.

All things are uncertain.

What is my condition?

I have to be faithful to my condition.

There are two lives. There is the old one and the new one. The old one was impossible. I could not return to it. And like some ancient superstition of children, or of the childlike, I will refuse to talk about it and it will go away. It will evaporate. It will atrophy if it is not nourished by words and awareness.

Repeat: The old life was impossible.

I will, therefore, focus upon the here and now. And be faithful to my present condition.

Inside the room, there is nothing to read except for the Bible that Harlan gave me several months ago, and seventeen newspapers all dated between December 16, 1967, and January 3, 1968. My name appears in eleven of those newspapers. It is now May 15, 1968, and I am sitting here in this hot, cheap room, starting to write my story, because it has to be written, and I am probably the only person in the world who has known me over the last year or two who believes that I am not dead.

I once had a teacher in high school who urged all her students to write down their thoughts, because, she said, it is only through expression of some sort that things become entirely real for us, and all of us have valuable things to say. There was something unforgettable about her. She repeated this idealistic advice of hers again and again, and her influence among her students was so great that many of them—the girls especially—began to keep diaries and "journals" when they were in her class. Her name was Miss Temple, and she would often say that nothing was without importance, once you found the right and beautiful words for it.

As for me, these many years afterwards, I can't say that I am striving for anything beautiful, but I am concerned with finding the right words for what has happened to me. And I believe that Miss Temple was right,

4

and that the only way I can make sense out of the last seven months is to try to express what has happened. And try to express what is happening now, day by day, as I write about that other time, and how I got where I am now. To make words out of my memories, so that when I go to sleep at night, I will not invariably lie awake thinking of the river.

It has been exactly five months now.

Maybe I want it to be beautiful, too. I'm not sure.

Water can serve as a mirror.

Therefore, I am living on the other side of the looking glass. It is all strange and terrifying and beautiful. And ugly, too.

Where will I be tomorrow?

The thought of leaving again makes me tremble.

One thing I have to get straight and not forget, no matter what inconsistencies I'm trapped in: my salvation is here. I have to retain my job at the C. & J.

Yesterday was hot and muggy, and this morning was much the same. Only a slight shining morning quality upon things. It is Thursday.

I walked to the C. & J. Restaurant, noticing things as I passed them—the R. C. Cola sign that is rusting around the "C"; the empty poolroom, with its front window softened by a film of pale dust; Gain's Junk Store, with old Mrs. Gain sitting inside the front door; the Ingle Hollow Café, sighing long cool gusts of stale beer through the screen door.

And then the C. & J. Restaurant. It is just opening for breakfast trade. Charley, who is a widower, leans on the counter with his elbows, and reads a newspaper. He looks up and watches me come in. He nods at me, and I nod, too. For some reason, we don't speak to each other, although I believe there is respect between us.

Charley keeps a little garter snake in a Mason jar on one side of the cash register. On the other side is a little stack of pot holders crocheted by Billie Sue, one of the two waitresses. They sell for fifty cents.

There are a few customers already. Wanda walks swiftly through the swinging doors from the kitchen, carrying two plates of eggs, and calls out, "Hello there, Neil. You're kind of late, aintcha?"

I don't answer her, except to nod. She is a little, thick-legged woman thirty-eight years old, with round shoulders and a sunken chest. Her hair is dyed black, and she wears rimless glasses. I don't trust her, although she isn't impossible to get along with.

I remember one time shortly after I first started working there, Wanda leaned around my arm as I was washing dishes, and whispered, "Do you have a girl friend, Neil? How old are you, anyway?"

I just turned and stared at her, and she said, "I'll bet you're not a day over forty. Am I right?"

But I didn't answer that, either, and Wanda moved away so fast I thought she must have been angry. But later on, when I glanced at her as she was taking an order from two men, she winked at me.

The other full-time waitress is Billie Sue, who is a big, strapping woman of thirty-one, with crossed eyes, but with beautiful features and skin that is smooth and touched with gold. She never looks at a person, but always keeps her crossed eyes down, so you can't see them. A stranger might come in, have her for a waitress and leave the restaurant without knowing she has crossed eyes.

Billie Sue, lift up your crooked eyes. The world is so crooked, you might see more than we do.

Later on that morning, when I had caught up with the breakfast dishes and the lunch-hour rush hadn't started, I asked Wanda if Harlan had been around this morning.

"No, not that I know of," Wanda said. She was leaning back against the wooden chopping counter, smoking a cigarette with her arms crossed.

"What's Harlan mean to you, anyway?" she asked.

"You'd think Harlan was your daddy or something, the way you're always asking about him."

"Harlan is a good man," I said. "He's probably on a crusade."

"Good for what?" Wanda said, grinning and flicking her cigarette ash off so that it dribbled down the side of her dress.

"Not good *for* anything," I said. "Just good. A good man, and a real Christian."

"How old *is* Harlan, anyway?" Wanda asked, frowning. She considers age to be one of the prime facts concerning a person. If she finds someone who has the same birthday as hers—March 12, 1930, as she's told us all a dozen times—she is ready to throw a party, and she talks about it for days.

"Harlan must be seventy," I tell her.

"Well then he's plenty old enough to be your daddy," Wanda said. She went over to the sink, turned on the cold water tap and doused her cigarette out in it. "Because you aren't over forty, are you?"

When I didn't answer, Wanda dropped her cigarette in the trash barrel, and said, "What's such a big secret about your age, Neil? Everybody has to be a certain age, but you wouldn't think you were."

The cook, Mrs. Tarkington, came back in then and asked Wanda where the Ajax cleaner was, and if we should order more.

"How do I know," Wanda yelled. "That's not my job. That's yours, and Neil's here. You two know about that. All I am is a waitress."

"Well, I was just asking for information," Mrs. Tarkington said.

She is old and deaf, and almost a vegetable. Nobody talks to her, but she asks a question about twice a week.

They say the traffic was bumper to bumper. The New York *Times* said the bridge was seventeen hundred and fifty feet long, but they were wrong in New York. It was twenty-two hundred and thirty-five feet long.

Witnesses said it sounded like a jet breaking the sound barrier. A sonic boom. It was called silver because of the aluminum paint that was applied to it. It was the first of its kind in the world, with aluminum paint like that.

All is not well.

Harlan did not return from his crusade yesterday, but he came in today. I saw him in front, talking to Charley. His silver hair is long in back, curling over his collar. He is a little man, with a noble hawk-like face that you would think belonged to a giant, if you saw a photograph of his head alone. He holds his head high, and looks above the heads of others.

But his clothes are absurd on him—too large and hopelessly baggy, and sometimes he wears two or three pairs of trousers at the same time.

After he had talked with Charley awhile, he looked back toward the kitchen, and I heard him ask if Neil was there, and Charley said, yes I was.

So then Harlan came through the swinging doors, and stood there for a couple of seconds looking at me.

"Hello, Harlan," I said.

"Well, hello there, Neil," he said. Then he came over and I told him my hands were wet, so we couldn't shake hands.

"It isn't always necessary with friends," Harlan said. He has a way of relating the most casual or trivial utterance to some general truth. Sometimes it's silly, the way Harlan does this; sometimes . . . I don't know. Sometimes, I think maybe that underneath all the ignorance and superstition I see in him, and underneath his ridiculous stance of clownlike dignity, Harlan is wise, or maybe some kind of saint, if there is such a thing. I don't know.

"How did it go yesterday?" I asked him.

Harlan sighed and ran his fingers through his hair. "Neil," he said, "it was hard. It was difficult. But I sat down and counted, and I calculate that yesterday and the day before, I passed out seventy-two pamphlets."

"That's a lot of salvation," I said, turning back to the sink. I was half sarcastic; but not over half.

After I said this, I could feel Harlan's silence. Even with my head turned away I could almost see him frowning at me, with his lips pursed in thought.

Then—as I knew he would—he corrected my statement: "That's a lot of *troubling,*" he said. "And *effort.* 'For strait is the gate, and narrow is the way, which leadeth into life, and few there be that find it!' But it is beyond any of us to know how much salvation is in it."

"Yes, Harlan," I said, closing my eyes.

"What's the matter?" Harlan said.

"Nothing's the matter," I said.

"Why are your eyes closed then? Do you have a headache, Neil?"

"No," I said.

Then I was surprised to hear Wanda speak. I hadn't realized she was even in the kitchen, let alone so near. "He won't tell you nothing, Harlan," she said. "Not if he ain't got a mind to. And he's always doing something crazy like that, standing around with his eyes closed, laughing out loud, and I don't know what all."

"You haven't been sick, have you, Neil?" Harlan asked.

"No," I said. "I haven't been drunk."

Careful. We need our euphemisms. If we can control our words, we can control our realities.

"No, he's been sober," Wanda said. "He's been a good boy."

"We are all children," Harlan said then. When I opened my eyes, he was frowning and looking at my feet, shaking his head back and forth.

"Especially men," Wanda said.

Several times today I smelled tar. I don't know where the odor comes from.

God, I'm tired. I feel like I'm moving deep under water, and others are unreal.

I'm not well.

But I mustn't neglect this diary.

I remember all the details from that time. The weather prediction printed in the evening paper the night before was a low of fifteen to twenty degrees, and cloudy. Of course, everyone who thought about it assumed it would warm up some during the day; but in any case, it was unlikely the river would freeze.

Today, Harlan was out again on one of his sad and lonely little crusades, distributing pamphlets. And the restaurant was very busy, for which fact I am glad. I enjoy washing dishes—having them come to me burdened with their filth and seeing them grow clean and shiny under my hands. This, too, is a kind of rebirth.

I was standing at the sink today, deep in thought, when I smelled a sudden whiff of cigarette smoke.

I turned around and saw Wanda standing right behind me, with her arms crossed and a cigarette pointing straight up between her fingers.

Wanda took a long drag on the cigarette, and then laughed a cloud of smoke. "Did you see her hair?" she said.

"Whose hair?" I asked.

"*Her* hair. Billie Sow's. Who else? Can you get over that big Billie Sow getting herself all fixed up at the beauty parlor?"

"Different people do different things," I said.

"That's for *damn* sure!" Wanda laughed. "You know something?"

"What?"

"I think Billie Sow's got one of her eyes on you. Which one, I'm not sure. You better watch out, if you got a weakness for big cross-eyed women!"

"Billie Sue is a good woman," I said.

"Good God Almighty," she gasped. "Maybe you *do* have a weakness for them!"

Mrs. Tarkington had an order ready for her then, and Wanda stubbed her cigarette out in a dirty saucer, and went to take out the order.

Billie Sue always brings coffee to me after the breakfast rush, when she isn't off work attending a funeral. I drink it, holding the cup in my slippery hands, and feeling the warmth of the cup. Is it from the coffee within, or from Billie Sue?

Billie Sue, you are a warm and silent garden.

And your hair is a flower.

And your skin sunlight.

Why should anybody care that your eyes aren't straight? It only proves that you live in two places at once, wherever you look.

Like all of us.

Sometimes, even after we close at ten o'clock, I return to the restaurant and stand there, longing to go back to work. Because work is now one of the few things that matter.

Harlan still hasn't returned from the crusade, distributing his pamphlets. These are pamphlets he himself writes, and then prints on his own little duplicating machine, which he keeps in his trailer.

Today, as I worked, I thought of Harlan. I thought of the first time we met, when I was sick and mortally tired from a long drunkenness. I must have stunk like a cesspool, and I was sitting in the C. & J. —this very restaurant— trying to drink a cup of coffee, which I held in both trembling hands.

Harlan came up to me then, and said, "I would like to give you this." He put one of his pamphlets in front of me, and I looked at it without reading.

"You're hungry, aren't you?" Harlan said.

When I didn't answer, he said, "It is no disgrace to be hungry, my friend. For we are all hungry, one and another."

I turned and looked at him then, and saw this funny-looking little old man with shoestrings tied around his wrists. His clothes were baggy and soiled. He had eyes that were deep and sad, and the angry, powerful face of a blue jay.

"We all hunger," Harlan said. "And thirst. And we long for rest."

Charley folded his newspaper up then, and came up to Harlan and said, "Don't waste your time on him, Harlan. He's drunk."

"He's hungry," Harlan said. "I know hunger when I see it, don't I? I know despair. I remember my Isaiah, and know the condition he speaks of: 'The whole head is sick, and the whole heart faint.' Let me buy a bowl of soup for him."

I shook my head then. "I can't eat," I said.

"Ah," Harlan said. "Hungry indeed."

"Leave him alone," Charley said. "You're wasting your time. Can't you see he's dirty drunk?"

"Hunger," Harlan said, in the voice of a preacher. "Hunger!"

Then Wanda came up and said, "Bullshit," and laughed.

I stared at her for a second, and then for the first time I saw the big one, Billie Sue. She was standing back at the rear, her body silent and calm, like a mountain. But her crossed eyes gave her face a bewildered, almost inhuman look.

I was to find out that it was rare to surprise her in the act of looking at you, for usually she kept her eyes cast down, as if she were ashamed. As I've mentioned.

"I'm going to kick him out before rush hour," Charley said. I looked at him then, and saw that he was a tall, thin man with skin the rich brown color of pumpkin and a strained-looking face—tendons standing out in the neck, an Adam's apple jutting out like an enormous knuckle, and veins and wrinkles all over his face.

"I'll take him back to the trailer with me," Harlan

said then. "He looks to me like a man in need of a friend."

So I walked with him up the street to the edge of town, where Harlan's old dented aluminum trailer stood, at the back of a vacant lot next to a shabby Texaco station. The trailer stood in grass as high as Harlan's waist, and bull thistles and wild maverick sunflowers taller than our heads.

The trailer was the strangest I had ever seen. Even in that first murky glimpse of it, I noticed that there were numbers painted in black all over the trailer.

This is where Harlan nursed me back to health. It was still the dead heart of winter, and I would sit there in the cold trailer and stare out at the gray town.

A few days later, I said, "It's ugly," and Harlan asked me what was ugly.

"Everything," I said. "The town, those buildings, the people."

"It doesn't make any difference," Harlan said then.

"Being ugly doesn't?"

"No," he said. "It doesn't make any difference where you are, or whether what you see is beautiful or ugly."

"To me it does," I said.

But already I had learned that this little man would never be drawn into argument. He merely asserted, without heat or anger, and ignored the comments of others when they didn't coincide with his own.

It must have been the second or third day, when I would go out occasionally for short walks, that I asked Harlan about the numbers painted in black all over his trailer.

"They're statistics," Harlan said.

"What of?" I asked.

For an instant, Harlan stared at me shrewdly without saying anything. In another man, I might have taken this for reluctance to speak, lest he be laughed at. But Harlan was impervious to the ridicule of others, and I knew that the shrewd look meant something else. Perhaps it was simply an appraisal of how apt I was in understanding the numbers and their purpose in being there.

Harlan finally answered, "Statistics of various things. Now this number, for example—" he pointed to the number 123—"is the combined age of my two grandfathers. One of them died of influenza at the age of fifty. And this is the height of the Empire State Building. And this is Noah's length of years, nine hundred and fifty. Here, the number of days in the year. Here, the distance from Salt Lake City to Providence, Rhode Island—cities I have visited in this very trailer."

And so he went on, his eyes sober, and enlarged by a sense of importance as he recited the numbers and told me what they meant.

One time this afternoon, I took a tray of clean glasses out to Charley. I noticed a stranger sitting at the counter. I could be imagining it, but it seemed to me that he was watching everything I did.

The restaurant was almost empty, and Charley was relaxing with a cigarette. He picked up the Mason jar with the garter snake in it, and said, "Neil, what should we name this little booger?"

I didn't look at the stranger, and I didn't look at Charley. I didn't answer, either. I squinted my eyes, and started putting the glasses back in place on the shelf. Upside down.

"Neil," Charley said, "why don't you give this here snake a name? He's a cute little fellow. Wanda said *you* should name it."

"What name do you like?" I asked him.

"Hell, man, that's what I'm asking *you*."

"All right," I said. "How about naming him Honor."

"Honor?" Charley said.

"That's right."

"That's a girl's name, ain't it?"

"How do you know the snake isn't a girl?" I said, glancing at him.

Charley's frown got deeper and he stared at the snake. Then he said, "Well, with a goddam snake, I don't suppose it makes much difference. But you can think of a better name than that, Neil. Come on!"

"Name him Caesar," I said.

I still didn't look at the stranger, because I was afraid that if our eyes met, he could tell everything, right away. Because I was sure the police had traced my car in Charleston, and this man was from one of the insurance companies.

"Do you think that's a good name?" Charley asked him.

"Sure," the man said. His voice was higher and softer than I would have guessed.

"How do you spell it?" Charley said.

So I spelled it to him several times, while he repeated the letters after me and printed the name on a three-by-five-inch card, using a cheap ball-point pen, with "C. & J. Restaurant" stamped on it.

He made the letters with slow, wavering strokes, in the manner of a semiliterate.

Charley is ignorant, like all of them here. No doubt of it.

Later on, I looked out from the kitchen, and saw that the stranger had left, and that the three-by-five card was Scotch-taped to the Mason jar. I couldn't read it from where I stood, though. I could hardly see the garter snake because of some clumps of long grass Charley had put in the jar.

What is it I want most of all?

It is honor. I want to live honorably.

I want to look in the mirror and see the face of a man anyone would accept and anyone would leave alone. I would want people to say, "There is a man of honor. You can tell it at a glance. Leave him alone. He is an honorable man, and a gentleman. He does his work and leaves others alone. And he is intelligent, with great strength in his hands."

No, no.

Honor is the main thing. I would sacrifice my hands. Not my mind, though, because intelligence is necessary for honor. You have to have an understanding of alternatives every time you choose, but always you choose the honorable one.

Therefore, you can't have honor without pain, and maybe a little sadness.

But honor is the thing.

I must stop repeating myself. I have to be more careful.

You can't have honor unless you are careful.

It requires subtlety to understand these things.

I mustn't be proud, though.

You can't be honorable with excessive pride.

Stop. Stop. Stop.

I have to remain faithful to the purpose

of this diary. Which means I have to write something each day.

So far, so good.

Later, I thought of what I might paint on such a trailer if I owned one: That there were two side spans, each three hundred and eighty feet long; and the main channel span was seven hundred feet long. The roadway was twenty-two feet wide, and the sidewalk was five feet six inches wide. Tensile strength of one hundred and fifty thousand pounds per square inch . . . far more than was thought necessary.

Was there anyone on the sidewalk? Could there have been?

This was something I couldn't possibly know. Or anyone else, for that matter.

My wife and children knew that I was driving a car.

My diary will surely take up more than one legal-sized tablet of lined paper. More than eight or ten, I suspect. Depending, of course.

Today, I almost left the C. & J. And yet, surely, this is strange to contemplate. When the thought crossed my mind, I trembled all over and closed my eyes.

It was Wanda who caused the trouble, of course.

She came up to me at the slack hour— about two thirty—and leaned her belly against my hips as I was washing dishes.

"Why don't you ever answer questions?" she asked. I turned halfway, so that I could see her out of the corner of my eye. But really, I was facing Billie Sue, who was leaning against the walls, with her arms crossed over her great warm bosom.

"Look at *me!*" Wanda hissed. "Not her. It's *me* that's talking to you, you crazy asshole. Not her!"

"I don't have anything to say," I told her.

"What you mean is, you don't *want* to answer no questions," Wanda said. "Come on and admit it. Come on!"

"All right," I said. "I admit it."

"Well, you can go to hell, too. Thanks a lot!"

I closed my eyes. "You're welcome," I said.

For a second, I could hear Wanda breathing hard behind my back, and then she thumped away without saying anything else.

A little later, Billie Sue came up to me and said, "Why don't you tell her something, just so she's satisfied. It don't have to be the truth."

I turned and looked at Billie Sue for a minute; I was surprised to see that she was staring at me. I looked in her good right eye while the left one stared off past her nose, as if ignoring me.

"I don't want to tell her anything," I said.

"*I* know that," Billie Sue whispered. "But she'll cause you trouble if you don't. You just wait and see. Wanda has to know about people. Otherwise, she thinks they're enemies."

I nodded, but I didn't answer her, and in a couple of seconds Billie Sue went away, too.

Billie Sue, that isn't what we wanted to talk about, is it?

Later that afternoon, I heard Wanda say to Charley, "The only one who can reason with him is Harlan."

"Don't be so goddam nosy," Charley told her.

I looked out through the window in the swinging door, and saw Wanda leaning her belly against the counter, wiping her rimless glasses with a napkin. Her eyes looked red and angry with her glasses off.

Charley seemed to be watching me very closely after that, in spite of the way he'd criticized Wanda for bothering me.

Once that afternoon I got terribly tired, and my arms and legs trembled. I had to hold on to the sink to keep from falling.

God help me!

Even as a child I ran away. Once my mother went into hysterics, and called the police, saying I had wandered off our lawn. It was a big lawn—almost what you would call an "estate." This was in late summer, under the afternoon sun, and I could hear the loud sawing of insects in the grass.

This may have been near the time of the kidnaping of the Lindbergh child. I remember being brought back home, and standing there under the high rafters of our living room, while my mother hugged me and smeared her warm tears all over my face and arms, and moaned and cried, asking me why I had wandered away.

I don't know what I told her. All I can remember are the questions.

And even as an adolescent. I remember running away from camp, once, at the age of fourteen. The highway patrol picked me up along the highway, and my father laughed about it, saying we had always had wanderlust in our blood. My family.

This seems to me, now, to have a built-in paradox, like the idea of Protestantism, or freedom, or human dignity, or God. Or maybe, even, the reality of the world we live in.

Even then I realized that we can always be better than we are. And, therefore, other than we are.

Careful. I must not write about anything beyond the bridge. That is to say, before it.

Nothing to report today. Which is a report in itself.

Everything seems hazy and unreal. I'm so tired. I have a strange taste in my mouth.

I think it's like mildew.

I saw a dead cat in the road after lunch. Down by the Texaco station, and near Harlan's trailer.

Work was slow today.

Charley's sister came in and helped out, so I had the afternoon off. She does this now and then, usually when one of us is absent. Or wants a day off.

Billie Sue never misses the funeral of a relative or friend. And sometimes she even goes to the funerals of total strangers, where she sits quietly and weeps. And presumably she derives from the whole dreary business some deep and obscure female satisfaction.

I sometimes think of her sitting there with her legs comfortably crossed and her flesh settled firmly in the pew or collapsible chair, while her crossed eyes fill with tears and she weeps sedately into a hankie.

Last week she took the afternoon off to go to the funeral of an old woman who had once bought a pot holder from her. Or at least, this is what Billie Sue had told us. She has a remarkable memory for such things, and Charley never questions her, because she's so dependable otherwise.

And his sister came down and waited on tables while Billie Sue was at the funeral.

But today, she just came walking in, and Charley came back to me and said, "Don't *you* never want any time off, Neil?"

I told him I did sometimes, and he said

his sister was there and could take over that afternoon, if I wanted to have some time off.

That was all right with me, but when I left the restaurant, I felt lost. I just wandered around a while, and then I went up past the Texaco station and Harlan's trailer, and walked until I came to an old railroad track that went up through the mountains.

The track is thick with weeds, and I don't think it's ever used these days.

I walked for a couple of hours, feeling my shoes crunch in the cinders, and feeling the weeds and wild grass scratch at my pant legs. Every now and then I would come across an old log cabin collapsing into the ground, or maybe an unpainted house standing high up on a cliff. The dogs would bark at me, and the sound of their barking would echo back from the other side of the valley.

After awhile, I got thirsty and stopped at a farmhouse and asked for a drink. They gave me one from the well, and four or five pale and dirty little kids stood there and watched me as I gulped the water. I could smell wild peppermint as I drank.

When I returned, I was stiff and tired from the walking. And hot, now that I was back in town. I walked past the C. & J. on the other side of the street, glancing over a couple of times. But nobody saw me.

I went to the poolroom and drank a bottle of beer while I watched the hunchback win three games of eight-ball in a row.

Then I came back to my room, where I am now writing this.

All the afternoon seems remote and unreal. Already, it exists in the past. It seems like something I did inside a little patch of light, while darkness was everywhere else.

Idea: Suppose light exists only where you look. How would you know otherwise?

Ridiculous.

I am tired, and I should go to sleep.

I have to get up early to go to work at the C. & J.

I'll bet they really need me. I'm a lot faster than Charley's sister, and I'll bet a dollar I get the silverware cleaner than she does.

Maybe tonight I'll dream of a bridge made out of silverware.

I get ridiculous ideas.

But I love everything around me, and find it all beautiful. The worn linoleum in the C. & J. kitchen, the garter snake, Mrs. Tarkington's awful silence, the great silent mountains, the dust and sunlight blowing in the street, Harlan's trailer, scrawled over with a thousand numbers. All of it. Beautiful.

Especially Billie Sue, standing before an open grave.

I feel enormously strong. I could tear this light cord in two, but I won't do it. Snap. Like a thread.

The greatest things are self-control and reason and love and honor.

I want to write that down on a separate sheet of paper, sometime, and Scotch-tape it above the sink, so I can look at it now and then.

Although I should express it more memorably, somehow.

We all need inspiring things to look at. And if we don't have them, we should insist on being nourished morally and aesthetically by the things around us. No matter how ugly.

This is heroic.

I'm so tired I can't hold my pen any longer. Good night.

Somehow, over these last two days, I have managed to retain my job. This thing started shortly before noon, on the twenty-eighth, during the slack time when I sometimes go out in back and stand in the sun.

This is what I did then. There is a broken cement retaining wall, waist-high, about eight or nine feet behind the restaurant. There is a broken yellow-brick walk back there, too; and against the back wall of the restaurant, our cans of garbage are lined up.

Since it is summer, I go back there often, while Wanda and Billie Sue work and fill up my trays with dirty dishes. I am fast enough to catch up with them. I am a good worker. Even drunk.

On the twenty-eighth I went back there and stood, smoking a cigarette and watching a dozen fat flies circle above the garbage cans. Behind the retaining wall, a hill goes up so abruptly, it is almost a cliff of clay and rock, bristling with scrub locust, sumac, ash, mountain cherry, and hickory, and thick with poison ivy.

I like to think of the poison ivy especially; because I believe that a man needs to see ugliness outside, to help counteract the pain and terror and the ugliness within. Also, as an emblem of these. Because we hunger for the tangible, always.

While I was standing there, I saw a little girl of about four or five, with hair that was absolutely white. An icy white, and she had blue eyes. She came up in the little parking lot that separates us from the Ingle Hollow Café, and just stood there in the cinders. We didn't speak.

Later on, she left and I made up my mind. I threw my cigarette against the cement wall. I walked up the street to the wine store, and bought two bottles of sauterne. They were ninety-four cents each.

Then I walked back to the C. & J. Restaurant, nodding to Mrs. Gain, who as usual sat just inside the shade in her junk store. It was hot, but overhead thick white clouds were floating toward the east, like great gobs of foam on an invisible river.

I remember vividly what it was all like. I remember everything. Even now I feel the warm wind on my bare arms. I remember remembering. One thing I remembered was reading in the newspaper that three couples had been married on the bridge, during its forty years of existence.

And that it was silver and vast. And every time you crossed it, you could feel it bounce with the weight of its traffic, like something monumentally alive and sentient.

I stood in back, feeling the sunlight blaze on my arms and face, and as I twisted the cap off the first bottle of wine, I was thinking that every single moment is a bridge. And that sometimes you can feel it quiver beneath your feet, and you hear static in the sounds of the world, and you understand that the sunlight itself is trembling upon your face and arms.

While underneath, there is nothing but the void—darkness and cold water. And that the great central span of seven hundred feet arched high over the channel of the river, and the channel at this place was between seventy and eighty feet deep; and skin divers claimed that even at high noon, there was no light in the bottom of this channel. That it was totally dark, and cold beyond conception.

Last night I had this dream, and all day I thought about it. I thought about it as I stood there at the sink, my wrists sunk in warm water. It occurs to me that washing dishes for my livelihood these days is the precisely right thing to do. The symbolically right thing. I stand there staring at the tilting, seesawing water. Most dishwashers presumably focus upon the silverware and plates in their hands, but I sometimes wash for an hour at a time, absorbed only in the water itself. Water is like something alive, for it moves and sparkles and catches light in a thousand unexpected ways—the way the mind catches impressions of the world. But it is, of course, the element of death. Deceptive.

However, today I was preoccupied and saw other things mirrored by the soapy and dirty water I work with. In a word, the dream.

In the dream, Wanda came up to me as I was doing precisely this thing—that is, washing dishes.

And as she has many times in actuality, in the dream she asked me, "Neil, how old are you?"

Her voice was strange, the way she asked it. It was a little bit like the voice on a tape recorder that has almost run down. The voice was dull and lazy, as if spoken through a yawn. Perhaps the way you would imagine a voice to sound deep under water.

Anyway, when she asked me how old I was in this dream, I answered, "Five months old. Exactly five months, as of the day I started to write my diary."

And Billie Sue was there, suddenly, the way people suddenly appear and then sometimes evaporate in a dream, and she said, "Do you keep a diary, Neil?"

I nodded, but it was a terrible effort, because my head felt incredibly heavy and stiff, as if it and my neck were hardening like cement.

"Ask Harlan," I told her.

"Oh, I believe you," Billie Sue said.

Then we were standing out in a high meadow some-place, and it was light in the immediate area where we were standing, but it was dark all around us.

"Isn't Harlan here?" I asked.

Billie Sue's face was covered with tears, and her eyes weren't crossed. She was staring right at me.

And then Harlan was there beside us, polishing his shoes. He was sitting in an old chair, and he was bent over his work so that all Billie Sue and I could see was the top of his head. The bald spot like a little island in a sea of tangled hair.

"I told her I was five months old, Harlan," I said. I tried to turn my head to look at him, because without appearing to move at all, he had shifted to the side.

"I don't know," Harlan said, with his face still hidden.

"Can't a man be born again?" I cried. I tried to yell this, but my voice was ridiculously weak and distant, like a forlorn call from a child drowning in a cistern.

Apparently Harlan heard me then, for he raised his

face and grinned. His eyes were hideously dark and slanted, and there were fangs distorting his mouth.

Then I heard thunder, and he disappeared.

And at this moment, I woke up and found that I was twisted in my bedclothes, crowded against the top of my bed, with my neck cramped. It was just beginning to rain, and a wind was blowing through the blind.

Once more it thundered, and I said to myself, "I am alone. This is where I am. And this is a summer storm."

Christ, I have energy! My hands are strong. And I lay in bed exercising them.

I know I could strangle someone with them. Easily. Maybe they could stab me or hit me with a hammer, but I'll bet I could take them with me. It wouldn't take long.

I shouldn't have this much energy at my age. It isn't natural. I either go too fast or too slow.

That's part of wisdom, knowing how fast to go, and when to go fast and when to go slow.

Sex isn't the problem now that it once was, and I am glad of that. I think I can understand more now, without that madness.

You live to understand things. Or maybe just to understand one thing, which I can't name yet.

I've missed another day, and this is something I must correct. I feel guilty about it, because it is a loss of self-control. No matter how trivial the act might seem to another, it is—after all—important.

I can still hear you, Miss Temple. You were a great woman, in your way.

But little has happened today.

Billie Sue brought me coffee after the breakfast rush—just the way she usually does—and I drank it and watched her move around the kitchen, helping Mrs. Tarkington for a few minutes.

I thought of her as she must have looked when she attended funerals. I thought of her in black, standing at the edge of a grave. And of her watching them shovel great glistening clods of red clay upon the vault, while little frogs are imprisoned deep down underneath. Along with the casket.

Later I got weak and closed my eyes and just stood there by the sink, until Wanda started whistling, and I opened them.

Once Billie Sue came up to me and said, "Neil, you don't eat enough to keep a bird alive."

"What kind of bird?"

Then I laughed.

It was probably too loud, because Billie Sue actually looked at me.

Usually, she just keeps her head down and takes her breath in quickly before she speaks. She has a low voice, and everything she says is like a whispered secret.

She's very strange, no doubt about it.

I can't hold my pen any longer, although I could wash dishes from now until doomsday.

Maybe I will.

Enough. Don't start saying things like that.

The end.

The end, I said. Now *mean* it!

Question to consider: Which is the greater wrong— to wrong another, or to complain of a wrong against yourself?

It is a fact that to complain to another is to wrong him, if he is at all sympathetic. And if he's not sympathetic, what would anyone accomplish by complaining to him in the first place?

Ponder this.

Why don't I stop? Didn't I say I was so tired I couldn't hold my pen any longer?

Can what I say be believed at all?

Everything is evidence.

I am not complaining. To complain is to commit dishonor.

There. That's simpler, after all.

The end.

This time I mean it.

There.

(By God, maybe I did mean it! There's something sad in that. And funny.)

As with everything else.

This entry grows beneath my writing hand like a

cancer. Does God commit cancer, the way humans commit dishonor?

This is ridiculous.

Why can't I stop?

There. I did.

I mean, I do.

I want to concentrate on reality, and I will write about something I did today, which I don't understand. I mean, I don't understand the moral character of the act, because it was ambiguous.

What I did was leave the C. & J. during the afternoon lull. This is before the dinner rush. It's all right for me to leave during the morning and afternoon lulls. That helps make up for a long work day, which bothers other people, but not me. Maybe you've noticed that I'm nervous and uneasy when I'm away from the restaurant for long.

I needed some razor blades, so I went to the five-and-ten store down the street to get a pack. And when I was inside, I noticed a big basket of things for sale. Mostly, they were bath and toilet articles. I saw some bath salts for fifty-nine cents. Normally they were ninety-eight cents, the sign said.

So I bought a package each for Wanda, Billie Sue, Mrs. Tarkington and Charley's sister.

It was a little bit strange, buying something so cheap and yet taking care not to spend too much. And to figure ahead on my week's expenses.

I am as poor now as I used to be rich. It is a funny feeling, and not all bad. Just strange.

Money has more meaning to me now,

than it did before. And I suppose this must be good, because people need more meaning always. Your hunger for meaning is seldom satiated.

I took the bath salts back to the C. & J. and passed them around to everybody, and Wanda said, "Why'd you do that, Neil? It ain't nobody's birthday."

Billie Sue didn't say anything at all, just kept her face down and blushed. Mrs. Tarkington couldn't seem to understand anything, and she put her box on a shelf behind the oven.

It was a screwy thing to do, and I didn't feel right about it afterward. Something was wrong.

Later on that day, Charley was staring at me, and he said, "Neil, you're a funny guy. But I do thank you for them bath salts you give me. I'll give them to my sister, and she'll probably like them."

What did I have in mind? Why did I do a crazy thing like that?

The only thing I can think of is this: I need this place, and I want them all to like me and leave me alone. I like working here, and being at peace.

I like being out of sight in the kitchen, busy with my dishes and cups and glasses, cleaning them again and again. I get so I know just about every cup by the chips and stains in it. The plates and saucers too, of course. The glasses are almost anonymous.

I suppose I just wanted them to like me, and that was foolish. Because you can't buy friendship. Any damned fool knows that.

Oh, yes. I almost forgot: I also got a ball-point pen for Harlan. He is always losing pens and pencils, so I didn't get him an expensive one. Not only that, I was almost out of money.

According to the original estimate, fifty to seventy-five people died. But of course, this was impossible to calculate with anything like accuracy until people were reported missing.

Soon, phone calls to sheriffs' offices and city police indicated that some husband or wife, or son or daughter who might have been crossing the river at that time . . . that such a one was overdue.

By December 17 a number of people were listed as missing. Enoch Biggs; James Vernon; Marybeth Nims, and her two children, ages two and six; Harlow Smith, nineteen, and his brother James, age not given. Dolores Yarnell, Ralph and Sandra Wilcox and Darrell and Irene Munson.

I know them all by heart. Milford Fisher and his three sons, ages five, nine and thirteen. Jim Reisinger, the driver of a truck loaded with giant spools of steel cable.

Are they all dead?

How many people in Point Pleasant and Gallipolis and Pomeroy and Uniontown and Middleport think about them? How many are thinking about them right now, as I write their names down on paper? Who could be as close to all of them—in this particular way—as I am at this moment? Who remembers all their names as I do?

And yet, so far as I can know, I have never seen one of them, have never talked to any of them or looked in their eyes with human recognition. They are only names to me in my ignorance. But I remember.

I remember every name. Along with another name I have not listed.

Witnesses said the bridge seemed to break first on the West Virginia side, and instantaneously curled to the side as it fell. The heavy steel framework and the released concrete flooring slabs roared down on top of the vehicles, and all went down together.

Governors Smith and Rhodes were both on the scene by 9:00 P.M. that evening.

Eyewitnesses estimated that there were approximately seventy-five cars and trucks on the bridge at the time of its collapse. They were waiting bumper to bumper. It was at the height of the rush hour, with many people returning home from work.

When it collapsed, it made a sound like some vast explosion. It actually seemed to burst, rather than collapse.

A trailer truck was seen to float several hundred yards down the swollen river before it sank. The screams of the victims could be heard by those waiting on the shore.

Sometimes at night I lie half-awake and half-asleep and I imagine I can still hear them screaming. Question: How many others can still hear it? I think the screams were probably those of both men and women, such a sudden and unexpected terror as this reducing them all to a common, ungendered, childlike humanity.

As Harlan truly says, we are all children.

If this is true, then I have heard dying children scream.

All except one, who waited and watched and never returned to the futile, impossible life he had known.

There are some things that cannot be said outright. There are some words that cannot fit together. When they start to form in my mind, I hear a roaring sound. And all I can see is black water, and I feel a deep, silent coldness go through me like a deadly winter rain falling through the silver branches of a frozen tree.

Tonight at closing time, when I was sweeping up the way I usually do, I noticed that Charley was standing there by the door watching me.

Finally, he said, "Neil, ain't you *never* going home?"

"I'm not in any hurry," I told him.

"Man," he said, "you're always doing this. The trouble with you is you like that pissy-ass job of yours *too* much!"

It was a strange way for an employer to talk, and I didn't answer him because I didn't think it would be a good idea to let him know how right he was and how important the job was to me.

For a second, I just stood there with my eyes closed and waited.

When I opened them, Charley shook his head, said good night and motioned with his thumb for me to leave.

I leaned the broom in the corner, behind the door in the kitchen.

Wanda says that Billie Sue believes it's bad luck to step over a broom on the floor. She laughs at the poor girl's superstitions all the time.

Harlan believes that devils and demons exist. He believes in them literally, and says there is no other explanation.

Naturally, he quotes the Bible to prove his point. He has a mind that is strangely computerized upon Scripture, and almost anything that happens to him can be coded in Biblical language. Which act always seems to comfort him. And fascinates me, for some reason, because . . . well, I don't know why. Anyone with a strange belief or strange fancies harmonizes with something deep in myself. And no matter how silly the belief, I want to hear it spoken of. And I want more.

But Harlan's literal belief in devils and demons is something special. And it deserves to be recorded.

I remember it was shortly before I left the trailer to rent the room I have now. It was a strangely warm and sunny day, and Harlan and I were outside the trailer. I was standing in the weeds, and Harlan was sitting on the trailer step, with his elbows on his knees and his face raised into the sunlight.

He was talking about going on a crusade. He said that this was getting to be crusading weather.

I remember that a semi-trailer loaded with scrap metal came roaring over the hill beyond the Texaco station, and something was said—I don't remember what it was, exactly—and then we started speaking of devils.

"How can you say they exist?" I asked him. "Most people stopped believing in that sort of thing a hundred years ago. At least."

"That doesn't have anything to do with the truth," Harlan said.

"Well, maybe not. But you'll have to admit it's strange."

"People don't want to understand the strangeness in themselves. Not only that, are you sure they're all people?"

"What do you mean by that?"

"What I mean is this," Harlan said, lowering his face and contemplating his hands. He sighed, as if from the burden of revealing too horrible a fact.

"What I mean is, devils and demons pose as human beings. How else could they do the harm they do?"

"You don't mean that!" I said.

"Ah, but I do mean it, indeed and in truth. Nobody can say who it is, or even when. Because it's possible for all of us to be possessed at times, and be none the wiser. In some people, they have taken permanent residence. They reside there and work their diabolical business with none of us understanding what is happening. They might be glossy with power and fat with distinction. But they don't have souls, or else their souls are drowned in the stinking cesspools of corruption."

"How many do you figure are like this?"

"Maybe the majority. I don't know. That's something I'm not qualified to say."

"But how are you qualified to say the other?" I asked.

"How can you say that lemons are sour or pork tastes salty?" Harlan asked, holding his hands up before him as if measuring a fish he had caught.

"How can you tell them when you see them?"

"How can you tell that lemons are sour or pork tastes salty?" he repeated, shaking his head as if with the enormity of his realization.

I closed my eyes and laughed, and Harlan started humming "The Old Rugged Cross."

This must have been only a day or two before I rented my own room, and left the poor old lunatic to himself.

Wanda always moves swiftly. Sweat breaks out on her upper lip during the breakfast rush, and it stays there all day. She isn't clean, and when she hugs me, reaching armloads of dishes around my waist to put them in the draining rack, I can smell her body.

Always, she manages to say something; whereas Billie Sue, who wears perfume and moves slowly and carefully, as if her crossed eyes might at any moment wreck her upon some shoal, seldom speaks. And when she does speak, it is usually something practical—whether I want her to put the dishes here or there, or if I have more silverware ready.

One day Wanda came up, after having a fight with Charley, and said, "Did you ever notice how much of that stinking perfume she wears?"

I simply turned around to look at her.

"You won't answer, will you?" Wanda said. "You kind of like that big fat tub of cross-eyed shit, don't you? Her and her pot warmers and funerals! Me, I like to have fun. That's the kind of person *I* am!"

She hurried away with an order from Mrs. Tarkington, but a few minutes later, she pressed her flat chest up against my back and said, "Me, I don't like to wear perfume. If people don't like me the way I am, and the way nature made me, they can just leave me alone. Isn't that the way you feel about it, Neil?"

"People are different," I told her.

"That's for *damn* sure!" she said.

She took out another order then, and I was able to return to my dishes. I poured rinse water over a tray of water glasses. After rinsing them with two pitchers of water, they stood there neatly packed together, and gleaming in the dim light of the kitchen.

This was an elemental accomplishment, this cleaning. And I had known almost from the beginning that it would be my salvation.

I wondered if I could construct a model bridge out of knives and forks.

Even tonight, before I sat down to write this entry, I went back to the C. & J. and stood before the window in front. A soft night light gleamed at the rear. I could almost see the naked bulb in the kitchen that made the light.

I could see the dark outline of the cash register, and the shining of the aluminum strips along the counter, and the glass cases in back where we keep the dishes and water glasses, and the giant coffee urn at the rear, glowing like some metal cylinder under water. Sunken in the darkness like something in the water; or sunken in the darkness like something in the memory—distant in the past.

I didn't stand there too long, because it would attract attention from anyone coming out of the Ingle Hollow Café.

I thought of going in and having a drink there, at the Ingle Hollow, but I decided to come back to my room and write this.

Can you hear me when I whisper, Billie Sue?

Rock me, my sweet boat. Rock me.

Harlan has not returned yet. This is turning out to be one of his longest crusades.

Back when I was still living in the trailer with him, Harlan once told me that there is not only a heaven, but an infinite number of heavens. "When you go to heaven," he said, "you are still your old self. And that means you have to yearn and hunger. And that means there is another heaven you are yearning and hungering for. And when you go to this second heaven, there is still another; because the you that goes there is still the old you, and therefore tormented by hunger, or you couldn't even recognize it. It will always seek out a further heaven."

"What you are saying," I told him, "is that we are constantly being reborn. And all our lives *need* to be reborn. Is that it?"

Harlan frowned a little, but agreed that this was one way of looking at it.

"You wake up in the morning," I went on, "and you are reborn. The old you was drowned in the night, when you went to sleep."

Careful, I warned myself. Careful!

Harlan said yes, but it was a mystery. For how could you remember unless the you that remembered was still the same one.

"Doesn't Second Corinthians refer to a 'third Heaven'?" he asked, waving his index finger at me.

"I don't know," I said.

"Well, it does. Second Corinthians. Therefore, if there is a third Heaven, there is logically a second . . . and who's to say there is not equally a fourth and a fifth as well? I say there is. I say there is."

For some reason, I started to laugh then. It was a loud, nervous laugh, and I know it must have sounded odd, but Harlan was never bothered by it. I noticed that he frequently started to hum some old hymn or other when I suddenly laughed like this. It was almost as if he was joining in the laughter in some offbeat way. An obbligato for laughing.

It was shortly after this that I left the trailer and rented the room I have now. I know that I am not what most people would call normal, and I don't care; but Harlan is surely mad. He was never able, for example, to explain why he always tied shoestrings around his wrists.

All is not well.

I missed a day, and feel guilty.

This is foolish, but something is out of tune, somewhere.

People don't talk and look the same, somehow, and there are strange odors lying in the low places, where the sun can't reach.

All is not well. I keep saying this to myself, and then I correct my grammar. I suppose it's an idiom, but it isn't right. It doesn't mean what it is supposed to mean, according to the logic of grammar.

What it says, grammatically, is: "All is unwell." Everything is wrong. But what people usually mean by it is: "Not all is well." Most things might be well, but there is something wrong, somewhere.

This is more fearful and more insidious. If everything were wrong, you wouldn't really give a damn. But to know something is wrong within a context of right, and not be able to realize exactly what it is . . . this is bad.

Today I amused myself by thinking of things that are impossible to do.

Like, stand on your head and not think of strawberries.

Or, say the word "filibuster" thirteen times without thinking of fire plugs.

And, mind your own business without arousing curiosity.

Women especially. They're like horses. I once read that the Indians, when they couldn't catch one of their horses, would turn their backs on them, lean over and pluck some grass. The horses were so intrigued by this strange business, they would invariably come up and rub their nose against the warrior's back, and he would turn around and grab the horse's mane.

Oh, well.

At least I've written *something* today.

Therefore, I haven't lost control.

Billie Sue is like a Clydesdale mare. One of these days I'll whinny when she gets close to me and hands me my cup of coffee.

No doubt. She really likes me.

God only knows why. I'm worse than scum on the water.

And deathly tired, all of a sudden.

Sometimes fear rises in me like a cold moon, and I can see it reflected in the sewage of my thoughts.

Things are getting more and more tense. It's like the invisible screws that hold things together are being tightened too much by some terrible force.

I have told them very little, after all. Charley doesn't seem to care. I'm a good dishwasher, and that's that, so far as he's concerned. But I don't like the way he stares at me so much. Doesn't he think I do my job well? How could he think that?

Billie Sue doesn't seem bothered by my being an alien and a man without a tangible history. She is kind and unquestioning. As big as a boat. Most people would say stupid, but I don't think she is. Maybe it's because I like her.

Wanda is the obvious problem. Her foolish curiosity about the ages of people is only part of a deep and prurient passion to have information about them. Her obscenities and ugliness hide something deeper and less definite. She is vital and dangerous. Her thick fat legs pound her tiny feet at the linoleum as she works, and the sweat flashes on her upper lip. Her eyes shine behind her glasses, and her hair springs out around her head like a shapeless black wig.

Ninety per cent of our customers are regulars. But they're no problem, because usually I'm back at my sink washing dishes, and the only glimpse I get of them

—or they of me—is a rapid snapshot, now and then, as one of the girls bursts through the swinging doors.

My chief task now, as before, is to keep from betraying myself. Each day, I think, is one more remove from that time.

All of those who were killed and drowned surely wanted to live. And yet they died. While one man sat in his car, waiting to cross the bridge back into Ohio, and heard the sudden noise that everyone said was like an explosion or sonic boom, and he saw the third, or possibly the fourth car ahead of him simply disappear.

This man chose to die, you might say. To die, and yet not to die. Because when he woke up, he could still remember.

Therefore, he is now, at this time, already living in one of those heavens that Harlan has spoken of, and is now looking forward to still another, and hungry for it, where he will be further clarified and nourished. For this is still ignorance and hunger.

And now, as most men want time to slow down, this one wants it to go faster, because each day that passes carries him farther from that time.

For all his wealth, there was drunkenness and madness and apathy. A totally impossible life, and yet deep down underneath a little flame burning. A kind of pilot light hidden underneath a cold and empty furnace.

Ridiculous metaphor!

He was circumscribed and therefore imprisoned by all their expectations. Weakness?

Ridiculous question.

But true, in effect. An inert and meaningless existence, when deep in his heart he wanted honor and beauty and truth. Underneath everything.

How many people have this truth riding deep inside, like a small flowering of cancer?

Impossible. Impossible. Impossible.

Idea: The impossible is simply what you *call* impossible. Connected with a self-fulfilling prophecy.

But how would you ever go about silencing that voice in your head that keeps repeating the (impossible) word?

Yes, that's a problem.

"That's for *damn* sure!" as Charley would say, leaning over on the counter with his elbows on an opened newspaper.

His characteristic stance.

My characteristic stance: Standing in front of the sink, my eyes closed, bending a fork double.

Wanda's: Reaching around me and whispering poisonous questions in my ear.

Mrs. Tarkington's: Ambling sideways before the stove, like a great fleshy crab, dressed in a flower-print dress.

Billie Sue's: Bringing me a sandwich and looking to the side, showing only her profile.

The hunchback: Snaking the thirteen ball into the corner pocket, his eyes shining.

Evasive, as usual. I wander from the topic, with deadly intent. Right, Miss Temple?

The engine is running, and the heater is blowing hot air upon his ankles. He is waiting for two things: the traffic to move up the ramp onto the bridge, and for us to consider him once again.

A historical marker near the entrance, and right before the light, states that "Ohio" is an Iroquois word, meaning "beautiful river," and that La Salle was the first white man to explore it. This was in 1669–70, the marker says.

And sometimes he thinks that one of his children might be dead, or his wife. And he couldn't possibly know about it. Often, when I think about this, I break out laughing. It's an odd, crazy bark. I know that, but I have to do something or I'll do something even worse or maybe pass out.

Sometimes I do this as I am washing dishes and staring at the water, and when Wanda hears me, she shouts, "There he goes again!"

And then as often as not, she also begins to laugh.

We are all mad—Wanda, Harlan, Charley and myself. Even silent, patient Billie Sue, with her great female excess of flesh and her poor, pretty crossed eyes.

She was married once, but her husband died in a mine explosion.

If I had black paint and a brush, I would walk up to Harlan's trailer and stand there in the tall weeds and paint the number 103 on his trailer. That is the distance, by road, to the place where the bridge used to be. I counted up the individual mileages between towns on a road map from the Texaco station next to the trailer. That was about seven weeks ago, before I started keeping this diary.

Question: Is Wanda a demon?

There are two facts I have to conceal: that I have been rich—at least by their standards—and expensively educated.

The simplest method is silence, which comes naturally to me now. The most cruel demands made upon us, I sometimes think, are those that require us to speak. We are swept up in a current of noise and meaninglessness, but part of us always waits behind, crying out for us to return and listen to things other than human voices.

But I sometimes play games upon them, as well as myself, and tease them with hints of what I have come from.

Once, in the trailer, Harlan said, "You are an educated man, Neil. It shows in your speech."

When I didn't say anything to this, Harlan said, "Don't think I'm prying. I merely make the observation. Maybe it isn't needful for you to tell about yourself. So be it."

I remember that he was standing by his little coffee pot and staring out the rear window at a light snow falling when he said this. I was sitting on my bunk, only eight feet away, with my elbows on my knees.

"I went to college for a short while," Harlan said. "Although I can't lay claim to being an educated man. Not in the way you obviously are."

"What happened?" I asked him.

Harlan turned around so that the dim outside light framed his head, and his face was in darkness.

"I left for two reasons," Harlan said. "I ran out of money, and I found out that nobody there believed in the wickedness of man."

"Those were your two reasons?" I asked.

He nodded. "Those were my reasons."

"Why do you have to believe in man's wickedness?" I asked.

"Why? Because it's there. It's as obvious as a taste or a smell. But do you know why people don't choose to believe in it?"

"Because it's frightening," I said. "Or at least that's one reason."

"Yes," Harlan said. "That's one reason, but there's a greater one. You can't *explain* wickedness. Not even the Bible fully explains it. And if something can't be explained, you can't figure it out. And if you can't figure it out, it begins to grow hazy right before your eyes. And then, after a while, you say it's a ghost. And what do you say ghosts are, Neil?"

He was shaking his head back and forth in the way he has . . . a strange counterpoint to his speech, for when he is being most emphatic and most assertive, his head will shake back and forth, as if signifying disagreement, no matter what his mouth might be saying.

"I don't know," I said.

"They say ghosts are superstitions," Harlan said.

Then he poured coffee for both of us, and we sat there in the darkness of the trailer drinking it. The trailer was covered with numbers, and around Harlan's wrists, shoelaces were tied.

"And yet," he said after a few minutes' silence, "people hunger to believe in it. Yes, they hunger to believe in wickedness. For with wickedness comes the possibility of good. From these two, atonement comes. From the filth of our habitations and our ways, comes purity. And how could it come otherwise, except through corruption? How could it? I tell you, everything is holy."

As he sipped his coffee, he stared upward and outward, in the direction of the window. The light was murky and the trailer was cold. We were both wearing heavy coats in the trailer.

I've been expecting it. The day I saw that other stranger and named the snake . . . even then I was disturbed. And I shouldn't really have been surprised today, but I was. And alarmed.

The fact is, I carried something like eighty-two-thousand dollars' worth of life insurance, and they're not going to pay out that kind of money easily. Everyone might be convinced that my body is snagged somewhere down-river, seventy or eighty feet deep in the channel, but the insurance companies aren't going to give up easily.

Let's say, for example, that there are three bodies still not accounted for, after six months of dredging and dragging the river.

Isn't it a reasonable suspicion, at least, that possibly *one* of those bodies can never be found because *the person is still alive?*

How else would you explain the fact that even my car is still missing? The dredges have scoured the river bottom as far south as Gallipolis, and farther, and have salvaged cars that were mashed so flat by parts of the bridge falling on them at the instant of collapse, that the remains of passengers had to be riveted out and pieced together.

And eighty thousand dollars of insurance money will buy a lot of patience and cleverness, and a lot of curiosity.

Earl, I am speaking to you now from the Great Beyond. Yes, you son of a bitch, you were right. At least, the last part of what you said was right. We used to spend that much in two years, and my widow is probably still maintaining her queenly extravagances. But my estate will be worth seven or eight times that amount. Most of which I inherited, I'll have to admit. My parents always did spoil me, and gave me a great deal while they were alive.

God, how I miss that silly bitch!

I pray for her and the children every night. Even when I am drunk.

We are all mad. Make no mistake.

But I am wandering around too much.

What it was that bothered me this morning, was seeing this man I hadn't seen before. He was having a cup of coffee at the counter.

Wanda came back in the kitchen, waiting for two orders of bacon and eggs from Mrs. Tarkington, and she said to me, "I just wonder what that man's doing in this town. This is the third day he's been in here for coffee, and there ain't *nobody* knows what he's doing here."

I looked through the swinging doors, and saw him sitting there, calmly sipping his coffee. He was coatless, because of the heat, and he wore a short-sleeved white shirt with a tie. He had close-cropped gray hair, and wore horn-rimmed glasses.

For some reason, he just *looked* like an insurance man. Not a salesman, necessarily. A claims adjuster, perhaps; or an investigator of some kind.

"Maybe he's looking for you, Neil," Wanda said, on

her next trip out to the kitchen. "I'll bet you got a few things you want to forget in your past that you never talk about. How about it?"

"I'm forty-four," I said.

That stopped her, and she turned her head a little, and said, "Honest? Are you really forty-four?"

When I didn't answer right away, she slapped my leg with a towel, and said, "Neil, are you kidding me?"

"I never kid," I said.

"Shit!" she said. And then she bounded off again, with another order, and when the doors flapped open, I saw that the man was gone.

I stood there for a few minutes, licking my lips and trying to think of what I should do next.

Then Billie Sue came up, and said, "Neil, can I put these here dishes on the sink, or do you want me to pile them over there?"

I looked up then, and came awake. "Anywhere," I said.

"I just wanted to put them where they wouldn't be in the way," Billie Sue said.

Right then I made up my mind that if he shows up one more time, I will leave. I won't wait a second, or stop for anything. I'll go right out the back door, and step onto the weedy brick walk, into the cinder parking lot, and across it, past the Ingle Hollow Café. Then up in back, where there is an old rock stairway going up the hill toward an abandoned house. I will go up those stone steps and never show my nose around here again.

Even if I have to leave everything, including this diary.

If this happens, and you are reading it, you might find a clue in it as to where I intend to go next.

But then, maybe you won't care, unless you are an

insurance man and have the assignment of finding my whereabouts.

If you are, tell my wife and children that whether they can believe it or not, I love them. But I think there's something wrong with me, or I wouldn't have done the crazy thing I did.

Still, I can't bring myself to feeling sorry that I did it. Maybe that is the greatest indication that there's something wrong. I don't feel regret. Just fear, sometimes, and dismay. And this incredible yearning, sometimes, for I don't know what.

Harlan would call it a hunger, and I guess that's as good a word as any. I will hate to leave the C. & J., if I can't say good-by to Harlan and Billie Sue.

Of course, if you're reading this, you may not give a damn. And I can't blame you for that, either.

Who knows, maybe you're another one who's missing, and presumed dead.

There are six tables in a row. Rectangular green fields lying under clouds of tobacco smoke.

Along the edge near the entrance, there is a line of shoeshine chairs, perched almost as high as the dented tin moldings that border the ceiling. These chairs aren't used any more.

I like to sit in the end chair and watch the players and listen to them talk. I sit there like God above their contests, drinking a beer now and then, but seldom talking to any of them.

Sometimes I like to gaze at the old tin moldings. They are painted thickly, with ivory paint that has turned amber with age. They are filled with cherubic whorls and floral designs that are strangely incongruous in this room.

But no one else looks at them, so in a sense I possess them. This is the delight of secrecy.

Just as I am the only one who understands that Billie Sue is beautiful and fine, but very odd.

I sit up high, under the smoke, looking down upon the green tables and passing judgment upon the players, but also looking up at these designs now and then, and marveling at their tenacity in holding on without being observed.

This is exactly what I most admire.

This is honor. This is the essence of honor.

They all think I'm cracked, but I pay for whatever beer I drink and don't bother anyone, so they leave me alone.

One of the players fascinates me especially.

He is the hunchbacked dwarf, and his head barely reaches above the table. I marvel that he can see well enough to shoot. How can he triangulate and judge distances?

I don't know, but he does. I mean, he does manage to triangulate and judge distances. I don't mean that he knows, and I don't.

In fact, he is the best player in town. He ambles and drags himself about the table, waving the pool cue in arcs above his head, and squints and blasphemes and utters obscenities in a casual, brainless flood.

He is a walking sore of filth, and he drains abominations.

His eyes are slanted a little, and his nose is pointed like a carrot. His eloquent eyebrows rise in fine Mephistophelean arcs at every good shot made by another player, but the dwarf always wins in the end.

With each shot he calls, the expression is the same: "Nine ball pisses in the corner snatch."

No one notices his language.

But they stand in awe of the hunchback and his prowess. He is an angry little monster, but he is unbelievably efficient in what they all choose to regard as important.

I wouldn't be that hunchback for the world, and yet I do indeed pity him. Sometimes I try to imagine how he sleeps at night. It must be on the side. How else would he relieve himself of that enormous burden on his back?

The fact is, of course, that we are all children. And every time I see the hunchback, I see a wronged child. He was surely led to expect something other than this, I tell myself.

But there's no point in being sentimental.

I love this town, and am fascinated by all the wasted beauty I see around me.

Today, Billie Sue came up to me when I was standing at the sink, and said, "Neil, aren't you through there?"

Indeed, I was simply standing there, and there were no dishes to wash. I had gone through them quickly, turning them out in a blur of swift and efficient movements. I was sweating.

She laid two fingers on my wrist, and said, "Neil, I don't want to pry into your business the way Wanda does, but how come you don't never talk to nobody?"

I smelled her perfume when I turned around. Although she was sweating too. I could see little crescents of dampness under each of her armpits.

"I don't have anything to say," I told her.

"*Everybody* has something to say," Billie Sue murmured. (Did you hear that, Miss Temple?) Then Billie Sue's crossed eyes flashed past my face, and she started wiping the palms of her hands on her great warm thighs. She appeared to be a little unstrung by her own boldness.

I was thinking later: If I had been talkative, she would never have approached me like that.

Idea: We have to make the occasions of our lives serve us. And we are, therefore, responsible for our occasions.

How subtly have we created the situations we find ourselves in!

The problem is not just to create our situations (or to participate in their creations—this is more accurate, of course); we do this unconsciously, beneath our awareness, and thus are imprisoned by our own unconscious drives.

No, the critical thing is to *re*-create our situations. Explore the implications of that word.

Thus, we approach every event in the spirit of re-creation. And conversely are re-created by the things about us.

This is important.

I'll have to come back and read this again and again, and try to understand all the implications in it.

But isn't this the same as rebirth? I mean, isn't re-creation the same?

If I had been any different—if I had varied in the slightest way from what I was—I wouldn't have turned back at the bridge.

But mental trouble and drinking and the old, compulsive evil of that other life. And there I was when the bridge fell, and it was like an act of God. Like a divine invitation to begin again.

"Be re-created," the bridge commanded me.

"Do you mean, be amused?" I asked it.

"No," the bridge said. "You understand. Don't try to be witty with me."

That's what the bridge said, and I said, yes.

"All right," I said.

I heard it, all right.

It would take a madman to do what I did.

It's no wonder this diary is so crazy, and that I stand before the sink with my eyes closed.

I feel sorry for everyone around me.

I tell you, I would be terrified if someone like me were around all the time.

Why do I act the way I do? And why do I think all these things?

I want to believe them, that's why. I want to believe superstitions and madnesses so they can insulate the truth, which I never forget.

Don't be conceited, Neil.

Billie Sue brought me a sandwich and coffee for lunch today, and she said I ate like a bird.

When she said this, I got a quick glimpse of pigeons flying high above the river, looking for their nests.

I laughed at the thought of them. Who knows, maybe they're still flying!

They're probably about one hundred and fifty feet up in the air. No, more likely two hundred feet.

I think, upon reconsidering, that it's more likely about two hundred and seventy-five, or maybe three hundred. At least.

It is important to get the right measurements of things, and to make the right connections.

I swear, I am only concerned with the relevant.

Yes. That's it! The old life was irrelevant. That's the most damnable thing you could say about it.

Irrelevant and without honor.

I felt very strong today, and laughed at the thought of the birds. I could have snapped the knives and forks in two, if I'd wanted to do such a crazy and destructive thing.

Later, I felt sorry for them, and a terrible weakness came over me. Wanda said something to me, but I couldn't hear what she said.

Sometimes I think I'm deaf and dumb.

Along with crazy.

Actually, I'd say my appetite is a little better than average. I eat quite a lot.

Sometimes I snatch the remains of a sandwich off a saucer when no one is looking, and gulp it down.

Wanda came up to me after breakfast and whispered, "Charley's drunk. Christ, you ought to see him!"

When she went back out, I got a glimpse of him, sitting there at his own counter, smoking a cigarette with his arms stretched out before him on the counter. He turned around and gave me a long, sleepy drunken look, and then the doors whipped shut.

Billie Sue came back in a few minutes, and said, "Did you see Charley, Neil?"

"Yes, I saw him."

"Wanda and I are taking care of the cash register," she said. "Do you suppose you could help out?"

"Maybe," I said.

And a few minutes later, Billie Sue motioned for me that they needed help. It was the beginning of the lunch hour, and Charley had taken off. Maybe he was over at the Ingle Hollow, drinking some more.

I was a little uneasy there at the cash register, for fear the insurance man would come through the door. I kept trying to figure what I would do if he did come in. Charley kept a snub-nosed .38 revolver in the back part of the cash register drawer, and several times I fingered it. I saw it was loaded.

But he didn't come back, and along about one thirty, the crowd slowed up a little, and Mrs. Tarkington called out through the door that we didn't have any more clean silverware.

So I went back and started in on all the dishes and silverware that had accumulated. In a couple of minutes, I was soaked with perspiration, and my arms were trembling as I plunged my hands in the hot water.

Wanda came up then and shoved a cold bottle of beer in my face. "Go on," she said. "You been a good boy, and you deserve a little something from the Ingle Hollow for your extra work."

I drank from the bottle, and then asked Wanda if the strange man had returned.

"No," she said. "I think I know what he was doing here, though. He's probably one of them engineers from Charleston. They're down here looking at the place for a new bridge for the turnpike. Bruce Gilley told me."

I nodded and drank from my beer bottle.

About an hour ago it started raining, and it hasn't let up. My landlady, Mrs. Chapman, is downstairs. Wanda is home with her husband and her children. Billie Sue is home with her mother and father, a dozen miles up in the mountains. Charley is probably still drunk somewhere, or maybe home, sleeping it off.

The rain feels good. It's cooling off my room, which is usually too hot at night.

Harlan still hasn't returned. I wonder if he's all right. He's awfully old to be wandering around in this heat, and working as hard as he does, trying to save souls.

The damned ridiculous clown.

I haven't explained about the car, yet; and I should.

Afterward, this was the major problem.

For a while I thought it would be best to try to run it off the highway somewhere down-river, so that they would think it had been washed downstream from the bridge. In a catastrophe like this, I knew cars were likely to turn up almost any-where in the river, and in almost any kind of condition.

But this was impossible. The sheriff, or whoever first discovered the car, would be sure to see where it had been driven off the road. Unless I was lucky enough to hit the deep channel at that particular spot, and the car would sink out of sight.

There was a chance of this, naturally, and a pretty good one, because the river is deep. But I didn't know the Ohio, and didn't have any idea of how the channel ran.

Whatever I decided, I had to act quickly.

I was driving south toward Charleston. I needed time to think. So I stopped at a roadside bar just outside the city and had a couple of drinks.

And it was while I was sitting there that I had an idea. I went outside, got into my car, and drove until I came to a hard-ware store on the outskirts of Charleston. It was in a shopping center, and it wasn't exactly a hardware store, but one of those big super-markets for general merchandise—everything from lawn sprinklers and hot-water heaters to popular records and Timex watches.

I bought a screw driver and a pair of pliers. Then I went back to my car, and drove it down into the city proper.

I stopped and got another drink or two, and by now I was drunk enough not to give a damn, but sober enough to remember what it was I had to do.

I drove along some of the darkest side streets I could find until I saw a car parked high up in a driveway beside a dark house. The house looked closed up. There were some big Norway spruce trees lining the drive, conceal-ing it from the neighbor's house, but a street lamp across the street gave me enough light to work by.

So I turned the lights off my own car, and drove up into the driveway, directly behind the other. Then I got out, took off the license plates and put them in my car.

The thing was not to hurry, so I slowly and carefully backed out of the drive and drove several streets away, where I stopped with the parking lights on and took my Ohio plates off and put the stolen West Virginia plates on.

When this was done, I drove along the river and threw the Ohio plates in.

All the while, I kept thinking of how impossible the old life had been, and how everything had pointed toward this day and this bridge. And how my wife and children would all be better off now, in spite of whatever shock and pain they might have to go through temporarily.

I went to a hotel and registered as Dan Hibberts, 122 Vista Drive, Huntington. I printed the name.

The next morning, I looked in the yellow pages until I found what I wanted, and then I took my car, with its stolen West Virginia license plates, to a firm that specialized in bodywork and painting, and told the man there that I wanted my pale tan Thunderbird painted a dark blue.

"Wasn't that awful about that bridge yesterday?" he said. "And all them people?"

I told him it was.

He showed me his color chart, and I picked out the shade I said I wanted. Then he told me his men wouldn't be able to get to the car until next Tuesday or Wednesday. I frowned, but said that would be all right; but that I would leave the car there in case they could get to it earlier. I told him I had another car I could use.

He said the car should be ready for me the following Thursday or Friday, but that I should call first.

I left the fictitious name and address I had used at the hotel with him, and told him I would call.

I left the ignition key, and walked out of his shop, with no idea of ever coming back to claim the car.

This was all very clever. It was only later I realized that if the man I talked to was honest, he would turn the car over to the police and they would check the registration number of the car and the key both, and be able to identify me as probably alive one day after the catastrophe.

But if he was dishonest, he might keep the car for several weeks and then sell it in some way.

Charley was back today, and nobody said anything about his being drunk. Everyone acted as if nothing had happened, which is the best way, it seems to me. Because we all have this deep need to erase things in our past. Or to be born again.

But yet to remain, and I suppose to have both—the rebirth and the history.

And in a similar way, I am not always intent upon concealing who and what I am. As I have mentioned, I play these wry little tricks—not just on others, but on myself, as well. Like most tricks people play, these are played on all of us. And even on you who are reading this. Whoever you are, you've got to enter into this in some way. How, I can't say, because I don't know enough about you. But I do know something about you, if you have read my diary this far.

So every life is an emblem, and it is meant to do two contrary things, conceal and reveal. And all our words are like this. And all our concealments have to do with erasing some part of our past, and all our revelations have to do with perpetuating this past. All of which happens in the present, which is the only place where the past can exist.

Little to report today.

I bent two spoons into complete rings, and then slid them into the wastebasket. Ashamed that someone might see them.

But I felt enormously strong, and what is strength without its manifestation? No different from ideas and feelings without their manifestations, which is to say, words.

Correct, Miss Temple?

Sometimes I wonder who is reading this. Not that I plan for anyone to read it, actually; but the minute I see words grow from beneath my pen, I cannot help thinking that they are speaking to someone else.

I think if I really believed this was all being written for my eyes alone—that I was simply talking to myself—I would confess to total madness.

As it is, I'm only a little bit wacky.

No doubt about that, Neil. No doubt at all.

No, sir.

So, let us assume you are reading this. It is inevitably true. The condition itself (the word "you") determines its own truth.

All logic is tautological, they say.

Whee!

I feel your breath warming the page.

For some reason the afternoon was especially slow today. I finished the lunch dishes before two o'clock, and went out in back and stood for a while, smoking a cigarette and staring at the flies as they circled above the garbage cans. Before I lit the cigarette, I could smell tar again.

I didn't see the white-haired girl.

Then I went back inside, and looked through the swinging doors. The restaurant was empty, but Wanda and Billie Sue were sitting at one of the tables. Billy Sue was holding Wanda's hand palm up, and saying something, and Charley was watching.

Wanda saw me, and said, "Hey, there's Neil. Come in here, Neil."

I walked in, and Wanda said, "Billie Sue's been reading my palm. Come over here and let her read yours."

Billie Sue had her face lowered, as usual, and she blushed as I came up. "I don't want to," she mumbled.

"Don't *want* to!" Wanda cried. "Why, you've *got* to! That's one way we can find out all about his secrets."

"Oh, I don't know," Billie Sue said. "Some people don't believe in it."

"Sit down," Wanda said, tugging at my pant leg. I sat down at the table, and Charley came over and said, "Where'd you ever learn to do them things, Billie Sue?"

"What things?" Billie Sue asked, still keeping her head down.

"Read palms, and things like that."

"Oh, Daddy told me a lot. And some other people."

"She's a real hillbilly," Wanda said, grabbing my hand. "Here. Read Neil's."

She took Billie Sue's hand and mine and put them together, saying, "Let's find out all his secrets, that he won't never tell nobody about."

Billie Sue looked at my hand a moment, and then flicked a look at my face to see if I minded.

"You don't mind, do you, Neil?" Wanda said. I shook my head no, and Wanda said, "See? He don't mind."

Billie Sue began to look at my hand. She put it out straight, and said, "The fingers don't fit too close together, so maybe he's a spendthrift. A little bit that way, but not much."

Then she bent my fingers back at the first joint and said, "Maybe he's a little bit stubborn. That's what it's supposed to mean when their fingers bend back like that."

She stopped then, and Wanda said, "What's the matter? You want both hands, the way you did with me?"

Billie Sue nodded, and Wanda said, "Give her your other hand there, Neil."

I put my other hand up, and Billie Sue put them both together, with the little fingers parallel and touching, and all the fingers pointing straight up.

"See the V the little fingers make where they go apart at the tips?" she said. "That means a person's either rich or going to be. Also, a hollow palm like he's got. That means you're going to be rich, too."

"Or *has* been rich," Wanda said, winking. "Right, Neil?"

"It don't tell about the past," Billie Sue said. "Except maybe in a way, because it tells you what a person is most likely to do. And that means the past."

"Look and see if he's a liar," Wanda said.

Billie Sue turned my hands over, palms down, and stared closely at my fingernails. "The number of white spots on your fingernails," she said slowly, after a few seconds, "is supposed to tell how many lies you've told."

"He ain't got hardly any," Wanda said. "I don't believe that."

"That's one old saying I don't put much stock in, either," Billie Sue said.

"I bet Charley's got a lot of them little white spots, don't you, Charley?" Wanda said, turning around in her chair.

Charley grinned and said, proudly, "I done told a couple lies in my day!"

Just then, two farmers came in, and Wanda said, "Oh, shit! Before we could even get started! You don't have any idea how much Billie Sue here can tell about a person from their hands. Are you really forty-four, Neil, or were you just kidding me the other day?"

"I never kid," I said.

Billie Sue got up to wait on the two farmers, and Wanda said, "I'll just bet you don't! Lemme look at your fingernails to see if you got any more of them white spots."

Wanda and I sat there at the table, while Billie Sue took the orders back to the kitchen. When she returned, Wanda said, "Billie Sue, what's one of them rhymes you told me once, about your hand itching?"

Billie Sue closed her eyes and recited,

> *"Left hand itches, rub it on wood!*
> *Wish for money, 'tis sure to come good."*

When she finished, Billie Sue said, "Not everybody believes in that, though."

"And what about the one about the mole on your neck?" Wanda said.

"Oh, that old thing," Billie Sue said. Then she recited,

> *"Mole on your neck,*
> *Money by the peck."*

Wanda turned around to me and said, "Neil, I'll betcha *you* got a mole on your neck."

"No, I don't," I said.

"Let's look, Billie Sue!" Wanda said. She stood up, but just then a fat woman with two kids came in, and Wanda went to wait on them. They just ordered Pepsis and a pack of Oreo crackers.

I went back to the kitchen and smoked another cigarette. Since there weren't any dirty dishes, I just stood there thinking.

A few minutes later, Charley came back and said he appreciated my taking over for him yesterday when he was drunk.

"One thing, though," he said. "That there gun of mine in the cash register. You know about it, don't you?"

"Sure," I said.

"Well, one thing: If some son of a bitch comes in here and tries to hold us up sometime when I ain't behind the counter, or if he causes too goddam much trouble, don't be afraid to use it."

"Sure," I said.

"Shoot him in the goddam head," Charley said. "This here's no different from Kentucky, in that respect. Ain't nobody going to fine you or put you behind bars for protecting yourself. So shoot 'em in the goddam head."

I told Charley I would, and he seemed a little friendlier than usual after that. He offered me a cigarette, and even though I had just put one out, I took it, and we stood there smoking together.

About a half hour later, we had a cold beer apiece from the Ingle Hollow. Then customers began arriving, and we were real busy until closing time.

I have skipped several days' entries, and this is bad.

A man must exercise control over himself if he desires honor. Next to language, our greatest invention is number. I only wish we could live up to it!

Harlan still hasn't come back, and I am afraid something is wrong.

I talked to Charley today and asked him if I could have a couple days off to go look for Harlan.

"Sure," Charley said. "You've already stayed here longer than just about any dishwasher I ever had. I can get me one of them winos from Ingle Hollow. They'll keep me in clean dishes. Or maybe Janet." That was his sister.

"This doesn't mean I want to quit," I said.

Billie Sue was standing right there next to me listening, and I thought I could feel her tense up at something in what we were saying.

But Charley didn't answer right away. He kind of stared way off through the front window, and then took a dime from a man for a cup of coffee and rung it up.

I knew he was playing some little game, but I couldn't help it—my hands started trembling and I felt like yelling out and breaking something.

But then Charley was staring at me, and he said, "Sure, I know that. You're not only the dishwasher I've had longest, you're the *best*. Still, if you want to take off, man, why there's not a blessed thing stopping you."

I nodded, and went back to my sink.

For some reason, I was still trembling. And then I realized that Billie Sue had come back and was standing there looking at me. Wanda was out in front, sitting down at a table with a woman friend and talking.

"Are you all right?" Billie Sue asked.

"Yes," I said. "I just got shaky, for some reason."

"Charley don't mean what he says, most of the time."

"That isn't it," I said. But I asked myself what Billie Sue would never be aggressive enough to ask: What *was* bothering me, if that wasn't it?

"I just had a chill," I said. "Right up along my spine."

"The old folks used to say that meant a rabbit was hopping over your grave," Billie Sue said. "But I don't believe all them things."

"I don't either," I said.

"You're tender-hearted," Billie Sue said. "I could tell when I read your hand. But I didn't say nothing, because of her out there. Her and her big loud bugle mouth!"

"What do you mean?" I asked.

"Your fourth finger is a lot shorter than your third. That's what that means. And I can tell that part is true, just from the way you act. You wouldn't hurt nobody if you could help it."

I looked at her then, and wished she would raise up her crooked eyes and look at me; but of course I didn't say anything.

For a few seconds, we just stood there; and for some damned reason, I thought of this thing I had heard or read someplace, and I told it to Billie Sue:

"If your foot itches, you're going to walk on strange ground."

"That's an old saying too," Billie Sue said. "Only some people says it's walk on your grave."

"Why are all those old sayings of yours so morbid?" I asked.

Billie Sue kind of shook her head and said she didn't know. Afterwards, it occurred to me that she probably didn't know what the word morbid meant.

I drank a couple of glasses of wine at the Ingle Hollow after work, and then bought a pint bottle of sauterne. Now I'm back in my room. I've just finished drinking two-thirds of a glass of the sauterne, but I still feel edgy.

Sometimes it's like I'm existing in this little square of light, and all around me is darkness and death. Life is only what I can see and touch.

But Harlan's out there in the dark somewhere, beyond, on a crusade, and he doesn't have a relative or anyone who gives a damn about him, except maybe myself. So I think I'll try to find him.

I don't know whether I'll get back or not. Things are too uncertain. Charley's reaction to my leaving was so strange and casual, it made me realize I'm nothing to anybody. Which I guess is what I've wanted for a long time, or how did I get where I am now?

I don't know. I don't know.

I'll leave my diary, because I can't go lugging it around with me.

The last I heard was that Harlan intended circulating his sermons up along the county road that runs past the abandoned house I mentioned earlier. It should be easy to pick up his trail.

I think I can borrow the car of a man I've talked to several times in the Ingle Hollow. It's an old clunker, a 1960 Ford, but it seems to work; and I've taken this man home twice when he was too drunk to drive, and put him to bed. He's a retired miner, and he's told me three or four times that he owes me a favor.

One thing I've proved these past few months: I'm no alcoholic. In spite of a couple of times when I lost everything and went blind drunk, I've come back each time, and gone for days, maybe even a week or two at a time, without anything to drink. Or without much.

Like this evening, for instance. That bottle of sauterne is in my chest of drawers, and I won't touch any more tonight. I don't want to touch it. For one thing, I want to be in good shape when I go look for that damned silly son of a bitch, Harlan.

Careful, careful.

I've got to change. As long as you can change, you're free. And who doesn't want to be free?

No, that's too complicated. It depends on the context. Freedom is my booze, in most contexts; and I am a drunk when it comes to freedom. Except you can have too much. I don't want to be free of the C. & J. That's an obvious truth I have to face.

I also have to stop referring to the bridge. I'll have to work at this, but nothing's worthwhile without effort, they say.

I've done pretty well in avoiding all mention of my life before the bridge. If I were to write about it now, it would flow back upon me, and I would be drowned in it.

All I have to keep reminding myself of is this: My life then was impossible, and we are all—my wife and children and myself—freer and stronger than we would have been otherwise.

I could have lived that life for another hundred years, and not learned anything. Without becoming a better man.

Once I was standing at the sink with my eyes closed, and Wanda came up to me and said, "Neil, just what do you think you're doing?"

"Nothing," I said. "I'm all caught up with the dishes. You haven't found any dirty ones, have you?"

"I ain't talking about the dishes," she said. "I'm talking about why you're standing there with your eyes closed."

"I'm thinking," I said.

"What are you thinking about?" she asked.

"Honor."

"What?"

"I said, I'm thinking about honor."

She was quiet a few seconds, and then she slapped a towel against my leg and said, "Neil, you got more shit than a Christmas turkey."

I didn't say anything, and she flicked the towel against my back and walked away.

She probably tells everything. To everybody.

I could strangle her with one hand and smoke a cigarette with the other.

But I shouldn't think such thoughts.

Because what we need to do is give things to others.

So later on, when the kitchen was empty, I slipped some money in Wanda's purse.

I wanted to put some in Mrs. Tarkington's purse, too, and of course in Billie Sue's.

But I didn't have a chance. We got busy and stayed busy.

Now, the stars are beautiful, and I am filled with peace to think that I gave Wanda something. Although it wasn't much.

Were these the actions of a man of honor?

Foolish, foolish, foolish.

Who talks about honor these days?

It makes no difference. Honor thrives most when it is most despised. It exists in secret, when no one else even thinks about it. This is its glory.

The night is beautiful and filled with a living silence. You can hear a great and powerful breathing underneath everything. I am filled with contentment and love.

My hands are strong, and I am at peace.

Can you hear me, Billie Sue?

Something is nudging deep underneath the mountain, and the mirror is ticking from some deep, unknown pressure. It will surely crack.

Behind the mirror, there is silver.

I am on the other side, and the real world is a memory.

It's late at night, and I am writing this in my room. It's a Sunday, so I don't suppose I was missed too much at the C. & J. They probably got along all right without me. All of us are expendable. Maybe Charley and Wanda and Billie Sue all got together while I was gone, and had a meeting, and decided not to invite me to come back to work.

In which case I don't know what will happen. Because I have to work. I have too much energy, and it isn't natural for a man of my age to have so much energy. Except sometimes I get terribly tired, compensating for the other times, I suppose.

I couldn't find Harlan.

Nobody seems to know where he is. I stopped at several farmhouses on the county road I mentioned earlier, and he had been at a couple of them, talking to the people.

But of course they didn't know where he'd gone from there.

The Ford worked all right, although it's in bad shape. Needs a valve job, I think. And a new muffler, I know.

All the way back, I kept thinking of Harlan lying in some field, dead. With his eyes open and sightless, each eye reflecting the full moon.

The moon *is* full now, and right before I got back in town, I passed the big abandoned house on the hill. I've mentioned this house before; you get to it up a long, crooked rock path behind the Ingle Hollow Café.

On the county road, you can see the slate roof of the house, as you turn down the mountain road that winds into town. Tonight, the roof was shining like ice in the moonlight, and the whole thing looked so lonely I could have cried.

That's something else that isn't normal. A man my age shouldn't be so close to tears so much of the time. I feel like a child, now and then, and it makes me angry to realize this.

No question about it—I'm not normal, sometimes.

But this doesn't always scare me so much, because what are the boundaries of the normal, if they aren't determined by the abnormal? I get this idea that normality or sanity—whatever you want to call it—is a little island in some great silent calm lake of madness. And the lake is filled with demons and sudden gusts of violence and terror.

If you have been swimming in this lake, as I have, you won't laugh. And you'll have learned to love that island where the sun shines and man is reasonable and kind. You'll love it in proportion to your understanding of its vulnerability . . . even its frailty.

Or maybe I should have said river, instead of lake. And maybe I should have written bridge, instead of island.

But then, bridge from what to what? From the past to the future? From death to life? From life to death? From the unknown to the unknown? The possibilities are too many.

My mind struggles and pants for air.

I'll say island.

When she came up with an armload of dishes, I stood aside and let her unload them for scraping. I noticed that her cheek and neck were faintly damp with perspiration, but only faintly. And I smelled her perfume.

My hands were damp, but I didn't care. I put them on each side of her thick waist, and the warmth of her body almost took my breath away. For an instant, I stood there, letting my hands sink deeper in her flesh. And then I pressed them lower, until I could feel the powerful female bastions of her hips, on each side beneath my hands.

For the merest second, I closed my eyes.

And then, Billie Sue moved away from me, without turning around. And of course without raising her head.

My hands were warm all afternoon from her.

And I wasn't sure she even felt me do this to her!

Ridiculous! Of course she did. Of course.

Billie Sue, raise your eyes. I am looking at you.

And can you hear me whispering as I stand there washing and rinsing the cups and silverware? Can you?

I am crazy to like her so much.

She is a cross-eyed widow. An ignorant

and superstitious hillbilly waitress who crochets pot holders to sell for fifty cents apiece.

I put quarters in the purses of all the women today, when they weren't looking.

I've discovered something: *We have to give things to one another.* If we don't, I think we might be destroyed.

No doubt about it: I do insane things all the time, and I can't seem to stop it.

God help me.

I don't want to lose my mind, whatever else happens.

Time flows in one direction, and no matter how much we zigzag, we are carried along by the current. And yet, life itself is the zigzagging.

The bridge was beautiful in the sunlight, and pigeons clattered their leathery wings like heavenly applause as they flew high among the great shining arches. For each pigeon, a quick reflection in the water far below.

A bridge is a place where two currents cross.

I must fight sadness and bitterness. These are weak self-indulgences. Nothing is so contemptible as a man who complains.

I love you, Billie Sue.

I am your crazy cross-minded child and lover.

Do you hear me when I whisper?

I can see you with my eyes closed. Sometimes better.

Have you noticed? We don't look at each other, Billie Sue.

We are the two who don't look at each other.

In the town's new poolroom, there is a hunchbacked dwarf who plays pool. He is the best player around here. His face is so low to the table, though, I wonder how he can triangulate his shots.

Strange.

Stop thinking about it. There are enough problems elsewhere. Leave the hunchback alone.

He doesn't talk to anybody, either.

We are all monsters. All of us.

It is Tuesday.

The little snake was found dead in its jar this morning. Wanda said she'd gotten attached to the little fellow, and was sorry it had died.

Last night, I dreamed of the pigeons. They say that on the next day there was a great flock of them flying in circles over the river, looking for the bridge. That's where they had nested for years, high up above, on the great silver spans.

They flew around and around, presumably bewildered at the disappearance of not only their nests, but the very world on which their nests had been fixed.

They say the two concrete supports stood there in the river like two great tombstones. They must have been shaped that way. I can see how people would think of tombstones.

Harlan is still gone. Sometimes I can see his body lying in the dark grass, his long silver hair mussed and his eyes rotting like jelly.

But I guess jelly can't rot, so I shouldn't write that.

It is important to clarify my language, because I am hungry for truth. Harlan was right. I say was, because I am certain he is dead. Who would know? Who would care?

That is the way I'll die. Like Harlan.

But I am avoiding what has to be told.

I am avoiding it, because it will be fearful to put it down on paper.

Yesterday, when I came back to the C. & J., my job was all right. They were waiting for me, and I belonged.

I was full of energy, and I worked like a madman all morning. I sang a couple of songs, making up the words as I sang, and several times I just broke out laughing.

When Wanda heard me once, she said, "There he goes again!" And she laughed too.

It was just like I had never been away from my job.

I know now, more than ever, that this is my salvation. I love to work here. I don't think anyone could understand how much I love this work.

I'm not sure, because I might have imagined it, but I think I stopped by in front of the C. & J. the night before, after being out all day looking for Harlan. If I'm right, I stood in front of the glass window and stared into the interior. At Charley's counter, and the cash register, where he keeps his .38. And the coffee urn.

Everything was dark and soft, as if sunk in water or time.

But I'm avoiding it again. Because I don't want to talk about it, and I'll admit I'm scared. My hand right now is beginning to tremble, and maybe the writing won't be legible.

I must not write any more about yesterday, but about today.

The truth has to be faced. Didn't I just say I was hungry for the truth? I will be consistent.

Charley came back right before the noon rush and said, "Neil, I want to talk to you for a minute."

"I've just got to rinse these saucers," I told him.

"No. Leave them be for a minute. And step out in back with me, will you?"

I began to tremble then, because I was thinking, "Oh, oh! This is it. They've had a meeting and decided they don't want me to work here any more. They don't think I'm good enough. I'm not getting the dishes and glasses clean. I'm sending the silverware trays out to them with the knives and forks encrusted, and the spoons filmed with yellow and gray poisons."

Oh, Billie Sue, do you hear me whispering my words to you?

You and I do not look at each other, Billie Sue. Therefore it is reasonable to suppose that we belong together.

You and I see two things at once. We are haunted.

Come near me, and let me sink my hands in your thick waist again, and feel the warmth of your heart that flows everywhere beneath your skin. You are a sleek mare, full of love and sweet grass, and your skin shines from within.

There are no clothes made that can hold all that warmth in.

You are my house, Billie Sue, where I long to dwell.

I love your clear brow and your heavy breasts. I love the great jugs of your hips and your white knees. I love your cheap perfume and your loused-up grammar. I love the cup warmed by your breath, and the spoon damp from your mouth. And your poor screwed-up eyes.

Careful, careful.

Stay away from me, Billie Sue.

I think I might be starting to smell of death and a cold river.

I followed Charley out in back, and we stood there in the sun. Charley offered me a cigarette, and I took it, even though I was so nervous I could hardly hold it in my hand.

"Isn't my work all right?" I asked him.

Charley had just lit both our cigarettes, and he shook out the match. One of his eyes was closed, because a thread of smoke was drifting up past it.

"Sure," he said. "Your work is just fine. Ain't nobody going to bump you out of that pissy-ass job, so quit your fretting. Dishwashing don't pay that much, even in this town."

"What is it, then?" I asked.

"Neil," Charley said. "It's just this. I know you been in trouble in the past. I ain't one to pry, but I can't help seeing what I see. And I know you been in trouble. You got all the marks."

He took a long drag of his cigarette, and stared up over the hill, somewhere above the abandoned house.

"What do you mean, all the marks?" I asked him.

"Never mind what I mean," Charley said. "Because I just plain don't give a damn what you done before you come here. I don't care who you killed, screwed or shit on. What I'm talking about is this guy who come in yesterday, asking for you."

"Who was it?" I asked.

"Some stranger. I seen him in here a couple times before. Wears glasses and he's got short gray hair. I figured maybe he was a cop."

I was so weak, I could hardly stand up. I kept staring at the flies, circling above the garbage cans, and I was thinking, "That's what we are. Flies, and filth. Filth and flies."

"Never mind arguing with me," Charley said. "Because I ain't about to ask you no questions. All I'm about to do is make you an offer. If you want to borrow my gun, you're welcome to it. I'll just turn my head, and if it's gone, I won't ask no questions."

I stared at him a minute, and I swear I thought his head was lopsided, like something melting in the heat. I licked my lips and tried to speak to him, to say something reasonable.

"Don't worry about me," he said. "I got me another one, just as damn good. So if that one is missing, I'll just put the other one in its place."

"Thanks," I finally said.

"Don't get me wrong," he went on. "I'm just *lending* you the gun. It ain't no gift."

"I know it," I said.

"And one more thing. A little advice. Don't run away. Get him now, before it's too late. Make it clean and quick. I know from experience, the longer you wait, the worse it'll be."

Flies and filth. Filth and flies.

That's what you become when you're dead. Unless you're drowned, and then something else happens if you don't come to the surface, all bloated like rotten melons and white as lard.

They say the current eventually wipes all the hair off your body, and even your clothes. So that you're naked and hairless and puffed up.

Or maybe I imagined that.

I can't write any more. I'm too weak and just plain scared.

God, don't let me drown!

Today I found out what his name is. It is Reynolds. Charley told me.

I don't know how Charley found out, but I believe him. There's no reason Charley should lie to me.

I wonder what Reynolds is doing now.

Maybe he's sitting in his room, as I am sitting in mine. Maybe he's having a drink in the Ingle Hollow, although I haven't seen him there.

He is the light, and I am the dark.

It's almost as if we need each other.

It's a strange game, whatever it might be called.

I have one eye that sees ugliness, and the other beauty. One sees darkness and the other sees light.

One eye is named Reynolds, and it is trying to see what was before the bridge, and it reads words written all over the things that stand in light, and the words exhort me to give in and return.

I close this eye as often as possible.

Billie Sue, both your eyes look out upon a world that is gentle and loving.

My sweet island. My sweet boat.

I must give things to people. What can I give?

Tomorrow is the Fourth of July, and the C. & J. will be closed. Charley brought in a flag that he is going to hang across the front window. And he'll put a sign on the door, that says, "Closed for the 4th. God bless America."

The word America is underlined, and I will be locked out. For a while, I thought I would ask him if I could come in alone, and just stay there. Even if no one else is here, let alone customers.

But he would realize how crazy I'm getting to be, if I said something like that.

For a while today I was standing leaning against the sink, with my eyes closed. And Wanda came up and yelled, "Will you look at that? He's *asleep!*"

Even Mrs. Tarkington heard her, she yelled it so loud. And Mrs. Tarkington said, "Maybe he's tired." And then both of them laughed.

Charley came back and said, "Remember what I told you, Neil. The offer still goes."

"Has he come back?" I asked.

Charley said he hadn't. And then I got so weak, I dropped a water glass, and it shattered in a thousand pieces.

Later on, I was washing a coffee cup, and I was aware of Billie Sue standing behind me. I turned around, and she was actually looking at me.

"You don't feel good, do you?" Billie Sue said.

"I'm just fine," I said. Only I really felt like I was going to vomit. I wanted to ask if he was out there in front, but I didn't.

"You've been washing that cup for about five minutes, Neil," she said. "I'm sure it's clean by now!"

Then I started to cry, and I said, "I don't want to get fired!"

Or it was something like that, only I'm not sure, because I was crying like a child and I couldn't see anything or even think straight.

I think she put her arm around me, but I didn't wait. I ran out the back door and walked around a while in back of the restaurant, sobbing and hitting myself in the face.

Pretty soon my face was all bloody, and blood was running and splattering all down my shirt and arms, and I was sitting on the ground.

"He's crazy," Wanda said. "The poor son of a bitch is *crazy!*"

I looked up, and saw all of them standing there, except for Mrs. Tarkington, who probably hadn't heard anything.

"Get him a bottle of beer, somebody," Wanda said.

Then Billie Sue started over to the Ingle Hollow, and Charley said, "What in the hell's come over you, Neil? Is it what we talked about?"

I wiped the blood off my face as well as I could. I had cut my lips, and they were beginning to swell. And I had cut my knuckles on my teeth.

"Something terrible might happen," I said. "We've got to be careful. All of us."

Billie Sue put a bottle of beer in my hand, and Wanda said, "He's like a little baby, ain't he?"

I shook my head no, and said, "You don't understand." And then I drank from the bottle of beer, tasting blood and beer all mixed together.

"Let's get back to work," Charley said. "He's going to be all right. He's probably been at that cheap wine again. Man, I'm a telling you, that'll *do* it!"

I'm still drunk and I can't hardly hold my pencil and I am sick and scared to death.
  I don't know where he is.
  I've got the gun.

I missed a day, and no wonder.

I hate to miss a day. This is my only salvation, this diary. Especially now that I'm not working any more at the C. & J.

I've got a little money, and I am now up in the old abandoned house, where nobody will think to look for me. Especially the gray-haired man.

Everyone wants salvation, so why should we pretend otherwise? Is it a loss of face or something, to want to be saved?

And it seems to me that being saved is tantamount to possessing the truth. If only for a few hours or a few minutes.

I keep thinking I am traveling toward the truth. That the river of time is carrying me toward it, and I won't even be able to escape it if I want to. I'll be carried over it, like an empty boat over a waterfall. Or some dam, which I can almost see in the moonlight, surrounded by dark trees. The water roars over the dam, not stopped by fear or hesitation, into some deeper level. And on and on. The water is silver in the moonlight. And nobody is there to see it.

It is breathtakingly beautiful. Lovely and silent. And pure.

But I am avoiding it, and it has to be said. That is, it has to be said and concealed, like the emblem of everything else.

What I did was take a blanket from

my room, the Bible that Harlan gave me, the seventeen newspapers, and the big tablets of lined paper, which constitute this diary.

It was after dark, and I carried everything along the hill in back. I could look down on the roof of the empty poolroom and Mrs. Gain's Junk Store, and the Ingle Hollow Café. I stopped right above the C. & J. Restaurant and caught my breath.

I was probably two hundred feet above it, and the lights of the street were on. And it all looked dim and dusty and pathetic. And hot.

Up here on the hill, it was cool. And there was a breeze, like the breath of God.

Ahead of me, and up above, the abandoned house stood. I couldn't see it yet.

But after a couple of minutes' walking, I saw it loom up suddenly like a great river boat out of the fog. It rocked there in the darkness before me.

Only the night was clear, and there was enough moonlight for me to pick my way along and up to the front porch.

I was careful not to trip over a loose board or step through a rotten place. The boards were gummy, and gave beneath my feet, like severed human limbs. There wasn't any glass left in the windows, and someone had tried to board them up, only whoever it was gave up after boarding up several of them.

I stepped around the house, and went in through the back door, which was stuck as solidly as if it had been nailed against the swelled-up kitchen floor.

The house smelled of mold and dust. And it was pitch black inside.

I took a few steps and threw the blanket down on

the floor. Then I lay down and prayed for a while. And finally went to sleep.

I'm not sure, but I think that was the night before last. If it wasn't, it was three days ago. In which case, this is July 7, instead of July 6.

I am proceeding on the assumption that this is July 6, however, because that seems more reasonable to me. Or more probable, I should say.

It is important for us to know the right time. Make no mistake. This is no triviality. Man needs his reason more than anything else, and time is an invention of the mind. A reasonable, and thus necessary, invention. Time is the only place where we can reasonably live.

God knows we need to know where we stand in the measure of time!

Yesterday, I drank the rest of a bottle of wine I had. There wasn't much, which is probably a blessing.

I went down after dark and filled the wine bottle with water from an outside tap, behind the Ingle Hollow Café. Nobody ever uses the tap. I wanted to go over and stare in the front window of the C. & J., but I knew better than that.

The Ingle Hollow was loud as usual—the jukebox turned up too loud and a gust of laughter blown through the ventilator now and then, as I stood there listening. My heart was beating fast, for I was afraid.

I will have to be an exile for a while.

But I don't want to leave this place. More than anything else, I want to come back to work at the sink. And just mind my own business.

That is, if I can keep from going crazy up here in this house.

It is very dirty and rickety, and everything is covered with a thick dust, which looks silver wherever the sunlight comes through the broken windows and falls upon it.

There is a filthy mattress lying on the floor in one of the bedrooms.

I slept beside it last night, but in my blanket on the floor.

The mattress is probably full of bugs.

Before I went to sleep, I could imagine a naked man and woman on it, rubbing each other and doing all sorts of obscene things.

The same old thing. The same old trap.

A man can live well and richly, I told myself. And he can be good. There is such a thing as being better than you might have been.

The old life held no promise. I was happy, but vapid. Is that the word?

Billie Sue, you are a testament. You are the word made flesh. You are an island of silence and health, and you breathe spices.

This morning I saw several cabbage butterflies whirling fuzzily and slowly about the yard, and I thought of the pigeons looking for the lost bridge.

Those pigeons are like our souls. This is something you've got to believe, whoever you are.

Good-by for today. Good-by. Good-by. Good-by.

Why do I repeat myself, when writing is such a pain in the ass?

Don't be vulgar.

Careful, careful.

Good-by for today.

I am sitting behind an upstairs window, looking down the rock path that leads to the back of the Ingle Hollow Café. I will write a few words and then look up, half expecting to see the gray-haired man walking toward my house.

It is late afternoon, and time hangs upon me like an enormous weight. A brutal collar of lead, gloves thick with gradually hardening cement, boots of cast iron. Time is age, and this is what we are faced with, you and I, and death, which you can hear rumbling over the distant mountains when the sheet lightning plays and flashes in the evening sky.

Beautiful!

For this heartbreak, that loveliness. For this pain, that ecstasy. All these transactions are taking place every moment, and we are all milling around deep down in the market place, somewhere below our convictions.

I love you, old house. Old aged mother, despised and forgotten. I love you, father mountains. Down below my feet, people are hiving like skinny sterile bees.

They are smoking cigarettes and taking deep drinks of beer in the Ingle Hollow and someone is standing in my place, before the sink in the C. & J., and Billie Sue and Wanda are whipping in and out the door.

In the front, Charley is taking care of

the counter and the cash register, now and then reaching far back in the drawer and gripping the handle of his other revolver. The empty Mason jar is on the shelf behind him.

Somewhere, a stocky man with glasses and a sun-tanned face and clipped gray hair is moseying around, looking.

My revolver is beside me on the floor.

Sitting here Indian fashion, which hurts the joints in my legs, I can look out the broken window of the house. All I can see are trees and the rock path, which is almost concealed by weeds and briers.

I can't see the roof of the Ingle Hollow or the roof of the C. & J.

Now and then, I can hear a hound dog howl and bark from somewhere on the hill behind and to my left.

The sound warms me, and I bless the dog, wishing only that I were as innocent and worthy of redemption.

Careful. It's unclean to feel guilty.

Time passes. Time is heavy.

Therefore, I don't sleep at night.

Which is just as well, because last night I did something important.

When I figured it was eleven o'clock, or later, I went down the rock path and stood behind the Ingle Hollow, where I waited for ten or fifteen minutes. I could smell tar again. Maybe the whole world is beginning to smell like tar.

This was Saturday night, and a dangerous time for me to be around here, but I had made up my mind about something, and I was going to go through with it.

What I did was go up the street about a hundred yards behind a building, wait until the street was clear of cars and pedestrians both, and then I darted across to the Texaco station. And then down the edge of the vacant lot to Harlan's trailer. It glowed in the darkness like a big water tank, and I couldn't see any of the numbers.

I had made up my mind to take his ditto machine, along with all the pamphlets and papers I could carry up to the house. Later, I would go get his typewriter, which he could barely use. He always typed with one finger.

I didn't want these things falling into someone else's hands, now that Harlan was gone. I didn't know of anybody who would even begin to understand Harlan and what he was trying to do. Let alone care.

The first thing that stopped me, was his door being unlocked. Usually, he kept the door locked, so people couldn't break in and steal his equipment—as cheap and crude as it was.

When I opened the door and stepped inside, I smelled stale wine fumes, and I heard a stirring sound beside me—like an animal moving in its stall—and then I was surprised by Harlan's choked voice saying, "Who is it? What are you doing here?"

"Harlan?" I said.

"Neil, is that you?"

"Yes. I didn't know you were back."

"I just got back," he said.

He struck a match and lit his kerosene lamp. I was surprised at the way he looked. He had a week's growth of beard, and his eyes were red and sore looking. And the shoestrings were still tied around his wrists. The trailer stank worse than the Ingle Hollow.

"I've been sick, Neil," he said.

115

"I see you have. And I can smell it, too."

"I heard you'd lit out somewhere," Harlan said. "Charley and Wanda told me."

"I don't want to talk about it," I said.

He stared at me a minute, and then he said, "Why do you have Charley's gun, Neil?"

I laid the gun down on the little shelf by the door, and said, "Harlan, I swear to God, I'm glad you're alive. I thought maybe you'd been killed or died or something."

"I almost was," Harlan said, closing his eyes and scratching his head. Then he stopped scratching, as if he'd heard a voice calling him, and he said in his Bible-quoting voice: " 'At the last, it biteth like a serpent, and stingeth like an adder.' Proverbs."

"Where were you, Harlan? I went out and looked for you last Monday, but I couldn't do any good."

"That's wine the Bible is talking about," he said. "And as for your question, I don't think I can answer it. 'The priest and the prophet have erred through strong drink, they are swallowed up of wine, they are out of the way through strong drink; they err in vision, they stumble in judgment.' Isaiah."

"Never mind the quotations," I said. "Are you all right?"

"No," Harlan said, standing up unsteadily and watching his feet as if they might betray him at any moment. "No. I am sick and fallen down in judgment. I err in vision, as the Book says."

"Do you want me to make some coffee?" I asked.

"No. I've got some more of that devilish wine. So let's drink that. How can you know bliss, without knowing hell? I ask you, Neil. You are an educated man. How can you answer that? The bottle is in that cabinet, there. I don't want to lean over because of my head."

I leaned over and got the bottle out. It was about three-quarters full.

"Take a drink," Harlan said. "Go on. Help yourself."

I took a drink, and Harlan quoted, " 'For all tables are full of vomit and filthiness, so that there is no place clean.' Isaiah is one of my most admired prophets. One of the very greatest. Great among the great."

I handed the bottle to Harlan, and he drank from it, wiping the neck with his sleeve when he'd finished.

"Great of the great," he repeated. "Furthermore, they say you should never look a cross-eyed person in the face, unless you take off your hat immediately afterward and spit in it. Otherwise, bad luck."

"Why'd you say that?" I asked.

"Because of that cross-eyed girl in the restaurant. She seems like a nice girl."

"What about her?"

"They say she was dropping things all day, the day after you left. And she cried, they say."

Harlan stumbled sideways as if the trailer had lurched, and then he drank again. "Oh, Neil," he cried, "I am a sick and stupid man! Grown old in my folly. I have a demon within!"

"What about her?"

"Billie Sue," he mumbled. "Yes, that's her name. Well, maybe she didn't exactly do what Wanda said, but she must have been upset the day after you had your spell, or whatever it was."

He handed me the bottle and I held it for a few seconds, trying to figure out what had happened. Then I took a drink.

"The other one," Harlan said, "said she was pining for you. Wanda. That's the other one's name. Wanda. She's a great tease, that girl! The cross-eyed girl almost turned inside out, the way Wanda was teasing her."

"Where'd you go?" I asked.

"Everywhere," Harlan said, throwing both his hands aside in a gesture of vast comprehension. "Everywhere and nowhere. Crusading. It's all the same. We are all visitors on earth. 'Who hath woe? Who hath sorrow? Who hath contentions? Who hath babbling? Who hath wounds without cause?' "

"What did she say about her?"

Harlan's eyes got big as he grabbed my arm, and continued his quotation in a hushed voice: " 'Who hath redness of eyes? They that tarry long at the wine; they that go to seek mixed wine.' Or is it 'unmixed wine' ?"

"I don't care what it is," I said.

"Her name was Billie Sue," Harlan said. "That's the one. People used to say a cross-eyed person brings bad luck, but I do honestly believe that that girl has a good heart. Isn't she a big one, though? And what wonderful tits! She isn't really what you'd call fat, but husky. Like a draft mare. Why, I believe she could break me in two with those arms of hers, if she had a mind to!"

I drank, and we talked on and on into the night, reciting drunken wisdom and nonsense, all snarled and tangled together like a backlash in a fishing reel.

When we finished the bottle, I realized I was still standing with my head bent under the roof of the trailer; and it was uncomfortably hot, and perspiration was pouring from me. I was drunker than Harlan by now, for I hadn't eaten in a long time.

He kept telling me to sit down, but for some reason

my legs wouldn't bend, and I remained standing. Harlan was sprawled back on his bunk, saying that we dwelt in the furnace of affliction, and quoting other passages from Scripture which I can't remember. Perhaps I didn't recognize them.

I would stand there for long periods, keeping my eyes closed and breathing deeply. Sometimes I thought I could smell tar. Sometimes I could hear Wanda say, "There he goes again!" and then hear the heavy swish of the doors as one of them took an order out.

Later on, Harlan heated a can of beans and frankfurters on his little burner, and we ate them.

Then Harlan told me of his old problem with drink, and how he had once, years ago, been a minister with a church and had suddenly begun to hear his own words mocking him. And he had begun to drink. His father had been a heavy drinker, he said, and he asked, "Should a man strive to excel his father?"

Harlan stopped his story here long enough to recite several verses from "Give Me That Old Time Religion," and then he continued with his story, telling about the time when he went to his church late at night, dead drunk, and passed out on the front pew.

"When I woke up," he said, "God's sunlight was streaming through the windows, pure and full of colors, like a waving flag. Outside, the birds were chirping and singing, bearing witness to the glory of the morning. And I was lying there, putrid and rotten with drink.

"I tell you, Neil, I arose at that moment, and the words from Obadiah went through my head. 'Though thou exalt thyself as an eagle, and though thou set thy nest among the stars, thence will I bring thee down.'

"And I scorned myself for my weakness and infidelity

to what I had sworn. And I walked out of that church and foreswore preaching from that day, because I no longer had the right to speak. And I didn't touch drink for years, until my children were grown and scattered here and there by their fortunes, and my wife died in a city hospital.

"Now you know why my heart went out to you that day, when I saw you. I could tell you were a man of intelligence and scruples, and were hungry as I was once."

"Now here you are again," I said.

"The wheel turns round and round," Harlan said.

I shook my head and tried to think straight. "It's late," I said. "It's awful late, Harlan."

But he felt in the mood to quote again: " 'Thine eyes shall behold strange women, and thine heart shall utter perverse things. Yea, thou shalt be as he that lieth down in the midst of the sea, or as he that lieth on the top of the mast. They have stricken me, thou shalt say, and I was not sick; they have beaten me, and I felt it not: when shall I awake? I will seek it yet again.' "

That night I slept on the floor of the trailer, and early in the morning, I woke up sick, and Harlan told me to eat some dry bread and the beans that were left in the pan.

It was almost light, but the street seemed empty, so I hurried across it, with my head down, and went along the hill in back until I got to the stone steps that climbed several hundred yards, winding here and there, until they got to the old house.

I wonder who ever built such a walk, and why.

Harlan had given me a can of beans. He insisted that I take them back with me, to wherever I was staying.

I didn't tell him where I was staying, and he didn't insist on finding out.

His eyes didn't look right, either.

God bless him, he was drowning. I could tell.

Now it is evening.

I don't know whether I can stand another night in this place.

The shadows are getting long, once again, and I know it is night coming on.

Harlan gave me some of his sermons, too. Which I stuck in my pockets, only I haven't looked at them. I will probably take them out tonight, when it's too dark to read.

That's the way I do things.

Beyond any doubt, I am truly crazy.

But I want to get as much down as possible, so that people won't think I am completely wicked.

I believe in wickedness. I can smell it in my breath, and even taste it, like something rotten inside.

I only wish I could bring life to someone, instead of death. Above everything else, I want to be moral.

My life is like the rocky path before this house, winding up some steep hill. The path is tangled and thick with weeds and poison ivy and prickly saplings. It reveals itself, and conceals. It flows and subsides. I look for allegories everywhere.

There is no bridge across it.

Enough. I talk too much.

Harlan is drowning. But then, who isn't?

This must be Monday. A beautiful bright morning.

Last evening, when it was too late to see my writing tablet clearly and I couldn't write about it, I imagined them again. I am speaking of the naked man and woman on the mattress.

. I watched them fornicate and whisper to each other, only I couldn't hear what they were saying. It was as if they couldn't see me, or know I was there.

All of this is ridiculous, of course, because I imagined them. And I *know* I imagined them.

Still, it was something to watch. I am lonely, God knows; but I don't like to feel sorry for myself. Self-pity is a disease of the worst sort, and it is filthy. Wrong. Worse than lying or deceit, worse than cowardice or hatred.

Worse than madness, even. And I should know.

Almost as bad as guilt, and related to guilt.

When I wrote that last sentence I was terrified that I would start laughing, but I didn't. And right now I am writing with complete self-control, and completely calm.

Sometimes—three or four times, I suppose (I wish I could count them exactly, but I can't)—I break out laughing. It sounds strange and totally insane in the empty house.

Sometimes when I take a nap, I imagine I can feel spiders weaving webs across my eyes and nostrils, and I wake up suddenly. There are a lot of spiders around.

I can't find my revolver. I don't know where I've put it, but I've got to find it.

Sometimes I walk around the house, saying, "Neil, Neil," as if I'm looking for myself.

This is so ridiculous that I wonder I can do it.

But I do it anyway, with a straight face, and not caring.

Christ, I'm nuttier than a fruitcake.

That's an expression we used to use as boys in high school. And college too, I guess. You don't hear it much any more, do you?

Who am I asking?

I am asking you.

It's hard to remember the boys and girls I went to high school with. It's surprising how many of their names melt in the element of time, and dissolve. Especially when you have known them at that critical time of life, when you are hardening (I mean that both ways) into what you will be.

Unless you are lucky enough to be reborn.

I can't remember their names, and even their faces are blurring. As a matter of inescapable fact, they are no clearer to me now than the faces of my two naked visitors who perform for me on the dirty mattress.

Or am *I* the visitor?

Today they even did it for me after a nap. Right in the shade, beside the great shelf of sunlight that slanted brokenly upon the dirty floor.

There's an old baby shoe in one of the rooms. I picked it up and held it for a while today, and then—realizing that the one who'd worn it might now be old or dead— I prayed for whoever it might be. Tears streamed down my face and into my beard. Do I still look stupid and evil? Have I learned anything, after all?

Whoever you are, you who are reading this (I'm getting lonelier, so you'll have to excuse my acting crazy now and then), can you teach me anything worthwhile?

What you can't seem to get through your head is how much I want to be good. I want to be moral. No, it's more than that. I want to be blessed.

What else is worth striving for?

I am hungry. That's what it is. Just as I am always trying to tell Harlan, only he won't believe me.

And speaking of him, he came up today.

It was quite a surprise. I was sitting there at the upstairs window, and I saw someone coming up the path.

Did I grab my gun then, and aim it? I can't remember. I'm not sure whether I had misplaced the gun by that time or not.

Anyway, I soon saw it was Harlan, and if I did have the gun in my hand at that moment, I surely put it down.

Harlan climbed the steep path a few steps at a time, and then stopped and panted. He had a big grocery sack in his arms, but it was only about half full. You could tell he was drowning. Panting for air, and his eyes dark as spiders in his face. The wrinkles in his pale face like scars, crudely stitched over to keep the face from falling at his feet, like a soft rubber mask.

Eventually, he came up to the porch. I heard him step onto the gummy boards and call my name.

So I went down, and he saw me, and I told him to come in.

"It's cool in here," he said, when he'd entered the house.

"Very pleasant," I said.

"Well, how are you?" he asked.

"I'm all right," I said. "But who told you I was here?"

"Nobody told me."

"Well, then, how did you find me?"

"I followed you as far as the Ingle Hollow when you left my trailer. And when I saw you go out behind, I figured this was where you were staying."

"Very clever," I said. "As clever as the serpent."

"I don't know what you mean by that, Neil," Harlan said.

I was sorry I had said it, then, and I felt the tears come to my eyes. This was a fine old man and full of silliness and zeal and ignorance and weakness. He didn't deserve my anger or my distrust. I am not *that* crazy, to think a thing like that.

"Have you read my pamphlets?" Harlan asked.

"No, I haven't," I told him.

"Neil," he said, "why haven't you? I think there are things in those little sermons that you will find useful. I say it without conceit, and in humility. For I think these things have been given me to understand, and the fact that I am ignorant and practically worthless gives evidence of the grace of God."

"And the arbitrariness of God," I said.

"Don't torment yourself like that," Harlan said. "You don't mean the words you speak."

"*Somebody* means them," I said. "Because the words come out. Therefore, they are caused. Maybe the words are given to me, just as your words are given to you."

That must have seemed blasphemous to him, but Harlan didn't let on. He merely shook his head back and forth.

"I am weak," he said, with a sigh. And no man's appearance has ever supported his speech more eloquently than Harlan's did then.

"I shouldn't have asked you to read my sermons," he went on. "That was vain of me, and we're all fat with vanity."

"If you want to know why I haven't read them," I said slowly, closing my eyes so that I couldn't see his face, "I'll tell you. I was afraid that if I read them I wouldn't agree with them. I wouldn't believe what you'd written. I don't think I could take any pleasure at all in that. There's been so much difficulty lately."

Harlan didn't say anything then. I opened my eyes and saw that he merely looked thoughtful.

After a few minutes, though, he held the sack out to me and said, "Here's some food I brought for you. Plus a can opener. There's another can of beans for you. It ain't much, Neil, but it'll keep you for a while. Until you cross whatever bridge it is you're trying to cross."

"I'm not trying to cross any bridge," I said.

"It was only a figure of speech," Harlan said.

I laughed and squeezed the sack under my arms.

"Is there anything more I can do?" Harlan said.

"No," I said. "But I do thank you. You're a good friend, Harlan."

Harlan kind of shook his head back and forth, and then stepped outside.

"Pray for me, Neil," he said.

Which surprised me quite a bit. Because surely it should be the other way around.

I took the food upstairs, and the naked man and woman were up there. They still pretended I wasn't there.

You could tell they were happy. Their faces were happy. And there weren't any lines in their faces. I could see only their profiles, however, because they never looked at me. I could see only her right and his left profile. Even when they turned in impossible ways, only those same profiles floated upon their bodies, happy and at peace. Even though the necks were broken.

It was obvious they weren't drowning. Of course, I imagined everything.

Later on I took a nap, but it was all like a nightmare. I kept trying to think of Harlan and dropping off to sleep.

I woke up and ate something, I forget what.

I almost put another entry in the diary, thinking this was a new morning. But then I realized it wasn't. That it was the same old day, and I hadn't been reborn at all. The air wasn't fresh, and you could tell it was afternoon.

God, you are more real to me now than anyone who has ever existed. Sustain me and make me strong.

The hound dog is barking on the other hill. Bless that innocent creature.

The cabbage butterflies are circling around and around, looking for their nests on the great silver spans below.

It is winter and dark. The naked man and woman stand before me, at least ten feet tall, their heads turned to the side. Their bodies glow silver in the darkness.

I am blessed.

Soft and tiny moths are resting on my arms. They are as thick as fur. In the distance I hear bees mumbling at some task, and I do not smell tar.

A temporary morgue was established at the National Guard headquarters. A New York Central commuter train conveyed people across the river only a hundred yards or so upriver from where the Silver Bridge had stood.

Right before you turned onto the bridge, from the West Virginia side, there was a traffic light. Sometimes I try to imagine that traffic light going on and on, changing from red to green to red, all through the darkest hours of the night. With no cars around, and with no bridge to turn onto. Just a ramp that rises and then disappears before the swift deep water of the river.

The superstructure snapped out of place so swiftly and with so little warning that live pigeons were caught in the collapsing girders, and were scissored apart and crushed by them. Survivors saw their bodies and fragments of their bodies—sometimes only little tufts of feathers—snagged here and there among the tangled remains of the superstructure.

I see it at midnight, the traffic light changing from green to red, and the colors reflected distantly in the dead eye of a pigeon. All around, there are girders tangled like clusters of tinsel fallen from some gigantic Christmas tree.

But I have promised myself I would not write about that again. You must forget the bridge itself to forget what you were before crossing it. Because in itself a bridge is nothing; its only justification lies in the twofold realities it brings together.

Is a man a bridge?

Of course, anything is a bridge that can be called a bridge. And anything can be called a bridge if it has something on both sides of it.

The secret number is three.

This is the number of a bridge.

Therefore, I will forget number one and number two. But how can you have number three, without one and two? Ridiculous, this whole obsession!

I thought I saw a little girl with white hair walk past the window today. But I didn't call out.

Last night I went down the path and stood in the woods there until two o'clock, when the Ingle Hollow closes.

I must have stood there for four or five hours, but I waited a little longer after it closed, until I was sure nobody was about.

Then I went up to the back door and hit the doorknob with a two-by-four plank until the lock broke.

I walked inside and through the storage room in back, and into the front part. The air was still full of the smell of beer and cigarette smoke.

I broke into the cigarette machine and took four or five packs and stuck them in my pockets. Then I went behind the bar and took some matches.

It was amazing how soft the noises seemed. Even banging away at that knob in back was quiet. I started out thinking, "This'll bring everybody running."

But then, after I hit the knob a few licks, I realized that the sounds I was making were really far away, and maybe even a little bit faint.

Then it occurred to me that I could even turn on the jukebox, and have a cold beer right there.

God, I was crazy!

And just in time, I realized that the jukebox would surely bring someone. I was disappointed, because I was lonely and wanted to hear some music. But there wasn't any reason I couldn't help myself to a beer, so I opened one and even poured it into a clean glass, and stood there drinking it.

I could see pretty well, because there are several beer signs in the Ingle Hollow that stay on all the time. One of them is a Schlitz sign, I think.

Only I'm not sure, because most of the time I was drinking that beer, I was standing there behind the bar staring at my image in the big blue mirror.

I couldn't get over it. I looked like Rip van Winkle. Or maybe some wild man in a circus.

I drank the beer and picked up an armful of wine bottles, without even looking to see what kind they were, and went out the back door.

Outside, it was cool and clear.

And the town was absolutely quiet as I climbed the rock path back up to my old house.

When I got inside, I sat down and drank about half of one of the bottles. Later on that night, I vomited.

The naked man and woman weren't there. But maybe they'll come back this afternoon.

It is now later, almost evening.

They did come back.

I'm drunk. I called out to them to turn around and look at me, but they didn't. Now I'm afraid that if they do, I'll find out they don't have any other side to their heads. That all they have is the profile I see, and the one eye and ear . . . and that the other side is hollow or empty, like the inside of a mold.

Maybe I am like God to them, and they can't hear me calling for them.

What are they saying to each other? I wish I were a lip reader, and I could tell.

I'm going back to sleep.

If I could find my revolver, I might kill myself. Although I don't believe in that kind of cowardice.

Still, you never know what is best.

A man is determined by the relation of what he remembers to what he forgets. I'm not sure, though; maybe he's simply expressed by this relation. Which would make all the difference in the world.

Obviously, it's both.

I've got to watch this tendency toward absolutes. Men drown themselves in absolutes, and don't even know they've drowned.

But do you see the implications? A diary such as this is an expression of memory; therefore, it is an expression and/or determination of what one insists upon being.

So this is why I will not write about my life before the bridge, because writing about it gives it a formal reality. Therefore, a power over me.

Do you understand me? Are you reading this, Miss Temple? You were a fine teacher.

But that is *exactly* what I said I wouldn't do! Miss Temple, you do not remember me, and I will not mention your name again.

Andy Detwiler, who was driving a big quarry truck heaped with gravel, went clear down to the bottom, he told a reporter. He said he felt the truck hit the bottom with all four wheels, and then the next thing he knew, he was on the surface —numb with the cold and soaked to the bone.

He said he was almost too weak and stunned to move, but somehow he managed to grab hold of a broken and splintered plank floating before him and hang there until some men in a boat pulled him out of the water.

This is the way it has been with me. Only I haven't gotten to the surface yet, but I surely have touched bottom, where there is neither light nor warmth.

Because I have been as insane as anyone can be. I don't see how you could be any crazier than I was.

Those words are more violent and more effective than "psychotic." Crazy. Insane.

I didn't really understand this, until last night. It was about dusk, and I came upon the naked woman huddled in the corner of one of the downstairs rooms. She was sitting there, crying, and right away I knew what was wrong. I knew exactly.

The man had left her.

Maybe she thought he was dead. Maybe she thought he had drowned while crossing a bridge coming home to her.

July
10

Who knows what she thought?

Of course, I was only imagining it, but I was lonely, and I didn't have control over what I was imagining.

Which might be like God, who imagined man. And, given omnipotence, merely imagining the existence of something is the same as creating it. And this would be a terrible fate. Because he, too, would not have control over everything that happened in his imagination, and we are all acting out fantasies in the mind of a neurotic God.

But this is part of the old craziness, and half of what I was thinking then, and half of what I am considering now.

Because, the fact is, we don't have control over what our reason tells us, either.

Careful.

This isn't what I wanted to write about, anyway.

I left the woman alone, weeping there in the corner, and I climbed the stairs, feeling terribly tired and sorry for her.

When I went to sleep that night, I listened, trying to hear the sound of her crying downstairs, but I couldn't.

Then I went to sleep, but I woke up in the night and heard a heavy rain falling on the roof, and saw a dim light shaking across the ceiling of the hallway. Then I heard footsteps coming up the stairs. They were slow and steady.

And then I heard a voice calling me, and I recognized the voice. It was Billie Sue's.

I stood up, and she came up onto the landing and stood there with a folded blanket under her arm, and a flashlight in one hand and a filled grocery sack in the other. I could see her crossed eyes clearly. She was a little wet from the rain, and she smelled of perfume. She was looking at me.

"My, you're a sight!" she said. "Are you all right?"

"Yes," I told her.

"I brought you some food."

"When is it?" I asked.

"When is what?"

"I mean now. When is it now?"

"It's Tuesday night," she said. "About eleven o'clock, I reckon. I just got off work and fixed you something to eat."

She laid the sack down, and then knelt and spread out the blanket and some paper napkins on top of it.

"My, but it's dirty in here," she said.

When everything was ready, and laid out, she motioned for me to sit down, and I did.

"Who told you where to find me?" I asked.

"Harlan did," she said. "He's planning to leave on another crusade, so he told me you were up here. He didn't tell nobody else. Just me."

"How about the one who was looking for me?" I asked.

"That man Reynolds?" she said. "He's gone. Charley told him you'd cleared out of town."

I was going to ask something else, but my mind was foggy and I was hungry. So I picked up a ham-and-cheese sandwich Billie Sue had made me.

She sat there on the blanket and watched me while I ate, and when I finished, we both lighted cigarettes. We could still hear the rain splattering on the roof, although it had subsided a little.

Then I asked her to tell me some of the old sayings she knew.

"About what?" she said.

"Oh, about anything. Do you know any that have to do with a bridge?"

"A bridge?"

"Yes. You know, something like, 'Never cross your bridges until you come to them,' or 'That's water under the bridge.' "

"Yes, I know them sayings," she said meditatively.

"Do you know any others?" I asked.

"Well," she said, "let me see. It seems to me there was one about a bridge. Something about . . . yes, I think I remember it: 'Footsteps are louder on a bridge than they are on the ground.' "

"I wonder what that's supposed to mean," I said. "Does it mean that emptiness makes more noise than fullness? Like a person with nothing important to say talks a lot, and someone with a lot to say keeps quiet?"

"I suppose it could mean that," Billie Sue said.

"Like Wanda," I said.

Billie Sue laughed and said, "Don't she have the biggest bugle mouth, though?"

"Or maybe it means that bridges are loud," I went on, "and give the impression that they're important, but they're not really. Every step you take is simply a step in some direction, neither more nor less, whether it's on a bridge or on dry land."

"I don't know," Billie Sue said. "I just remember all them old sayings, but I don't understand what all of them mean."

We were quiet a minute, and then I said, "What about spiders?"

"Well," she said, "if a spider drops down in front of you, you're supposed to receive a letter."

"How about snakes?"

"You sure are curious, aren't you?" she said. "Sometimes I have an idea you're just making fun of me."

I looked at her then, and saw her troubled face raised to mine. The light was just strong enough for me to see little curls in front of her ears, fastened there by light perspiration. Each of her crossed eyes was pretty and gentle. I couldn't help seeing this, although it must sound crazy.

"Listen," I said, lowering my voice as if someone might have heard, "that's not true. Honest!"

"I don't know," she said. "I just kind of wondered, the way you were asking about them sayings all the time. You and Wanda."

I crawled over to her on my hands and knees, and she said, "What are you doing?"

"I don't know," I said. But I put my arms around her and kissed her on the mouth, and then the eyes and ears, until she began to breathe hard and kiss me in turn, saying how much she had always wanted me to like her.

I put my hand inside her blouse and felt the heavy warmth of her breasts. Then I eased her back upon the blanket, and I said something about being dirty and crazy and not worth anything.

But she said she didn't care. And several times she groaned and pulled vaguely at my hair and whispered how much she loved me as I made love to her.

And how lonely she was.

Afterward, there was a sudden flash of lightning, revealing the high rectangular shape of the empty window, looking like a giant ice-cube tray, and the tip of the hickory limb outside. When the thunder followed, Billie Sue said, "That's the turtle letting go."

"What does that mean?" I asked.

She smiled and said it was a joke in her family, because there was this saying that a snapping turtle wouldn't let go his hold on something until it thundered.

And the rain reminded her of a lot of sayings about what will bring rain. Like, if you turn a dead snake on its back, it'll bring rain.

And then she told me several old sayings about snakes. Such as, if you dream of snakes, you have an enemy. Or, if you kill a snake, its mate will come to bite you.

Then she asked me again why I was so interested in those sayings, and I told her I wasn't sure.

She tidied up the room as best she could and got things as clean as possible with the handful of paper napkins she had brought from the restaurant.

Then we went to sleep together on the blanket.

Only before we went to sleep, I myself wondered why I should be so interested in these silly superstitions and Harlan's insane theology.

I couldn't figure it out, except for the possibility that I could feel a human breath in them. And I can't help feeling close to people who have long been dead, and have no other voice left.

This morning, before she left, Billie Sue said, "Neil, you can come back to work now. That man's gone away, like I told you last night. That man Reynolds, who was looking for you."

I didn't say anything, because I didn't know how much she knew. She was tidying things up—putting all the balled-up, dirty paper napkins in the grocery sack, and folding the blanket before her as she stood there in the fresh morning sunlight.

"You didn't kill nobody, did you?" she asked.

138

"No. Not exactly."

"That's all right. You don't have to tell me nothing. I guess I know enough about you already."

"Did anybody tell him anything?"

"Mr. Reynolds? No. Charley told him you'd cleared out of town, and that you'd probably gone over into Kentucky, or maybe down into Tennessee."

I think it was then I began to take hope. I felt strong and clearer in the head than I had felt in a long time. I kept saying to myself that it is indeed possible to do it. That you can, if you keep your head.

Billie Sue left me and returned to the C. & J. She said she would tell Charley that I was coming back, and I would be able to take up my job any time he needed me. She said that Charley's sister had been washing dishes since my absence, and she was anxious to quit as soon as possible.

The last two dishwashers before me had been fired for stealing.

I was going back to the C. & J.

I returned to my old room, which hadn't changed any, and which I had figured I might never see again.

I showered and shaved, and emerged cleansed of all the filth.

When I went back to the C. & J. at noon, everybody greeted me as if I really belonged. Wanda kept making jokes and Charley asked me where the revolver was, and I told him I would get it back to him the next day or so.

"No," he said. "Keep it around a while, in case that guy comes back looking for you with blood in his eye."

"I will," I said.

I was full of energy and worked too hard that afternoon, and was weak and trembly by evening. I wished

I had brought back one of the bottles of wine from the old house.

Billie Sue wouldn't look at me all day.

After work, I kissed her good night. She said she had to hurry home, up in the hills, because she hadn't been home the night before. She said she'd told her parents she was going to stay all night with Wanda.

Apparently she had already made up her mind about me.

When she left, she told me to take care of myself, and I said I would.

I went over to the Ingle Hollow and had a couple of beers. Some of the customers were still talking about the robbery a couple of nights back, and trying to figure out why no money was taken.

"He must have been a crazy son of a bitch, not to take no money," someone said.

"I don't care," Max Parker said. He is the owner and bartender both. "He done a hell of a lot of damage anyway. The next lock I get will be stouter. The son of a bitch who done it must have used a sledge hammer to break that last one!"

I felt proud when he said that.

I am very strong, there's no doubt about it.

I felt strong, then; not at all weak and trembling, the way I had a little while before.

Virtually indestructible.

When I went outside and walked home, I could smell tar.

Then, for the longest while, I couldn't think of Billie Sue's name. I mean, even her first name.

So I sat down and wrote this entry, which is one of the longest yet.

I'll have a hard time getting out of bed tomorrow. Sometimes it's like there's a wheelbarrow-load of rocks and dirt on my chest.

Why couldn't I remember her name?

There's no doubt about it. I am still crazy as hell.

Only it comes and goes.

Maybe that's the way with everybody.

I have to go to sleep. I can hardly sit up.

Only God knows how tired I am.

Charley was the one.

I thought it might be Harlan, first; or maybe even Wanda, with her itch to find out everything. But it was Charley, and I wasn't prepared for it at all.

But then I don't suppose I could have been prepared, no matter how it happened.

The day was hot again, with big fat cumulus clouds easing by overhead and boxing us in, now and then, with their great pressure. I could feel them overhead, when they passed. Even with my eyes closed. It was like my ears were almost stopped up.

You can walk around in the air and sunlight and still be drowning, and not even know it.

I noticed this early in the morning, when I was standing out in back, thinking. This was after the breakfast rush, when I was caught up.

Billie Sue hardly looked at me all morning, and hardly spoke. There is something wrong there, but I don't know what.

It's something I have said, or maybe something I haven't said.

What is it you want me to say to you, Billie Sue? What is it you expect me to do now?

Of course, I know what it is. Partly, at least. She's afraid I am going to leave.

What we must do is strive always to make the right connections.

After I got back to washing dishes, I remembered where I had left the revolver. It was in Harlan's trailer, when I'd gone down there to take his ditto machine, and had found him drunk in his cot.

Once today I looked through the swinging doors and saw Billie Sue crocheting her little pot holders. Her face was bent over, and I could almost imagine she was crying.

What have I done to you, Billie Sue?

I sneaked back and put all the change I had in my pocket into her purse. It wasn't much, only forty-three cents.

We should give things to one another.

Wanda was over at the counter, talking about her husband to one of her girl friends and Charley.

Charley came back to the kitchen and called for me. I could hear him from where I was standing outside in back. I could hear his voice above the whirring sound of the exhaust fan from the kitchen.

The white-haired girl wasn't anywhere around.

The flies were flying heavy and drunken, today. They looked different. One of the cans had been turned over in the night. It was either by a raccoon or some stray dog. There's no telling which.

But why should this matter?

Charley was still yelling for me. And then, he was yelling at Mrs. Tarkington— in a still louder voice—asking where I was.

Frequently, at such times, I see the world as something distant and inconceivably lovely. It is shrouded by mists that turn all colors into pastel shades.

You can feel it turning beneath your knees.

The world is a horse you ride, laughing in the wind.

Even the green flies are beautiful.

Even the pigeons, abandoned by their nests.

Even the cabbage butterflies, fumbling and fluttering at your ears as you drowse in the afternoon, and smile.

Saying yes. Yes. Yes.

Charley finally came out the back door, letting it slam so loudly that the flies lifted in unison, and then settled back.

Charley was holding some bent knives and forks and spoons in his hands.

"What's happening to our silverware?" he asked.

He held them all up in front of my face.

"Why are all these goddam knives and forks bent?" he asked.

"Spoons, too," I reminded him.

"Yes," he said. "Spoons, too."

"I don't know," I said.

"I've never seen nothing like it," Charley said, shaking his head back and forth, as if from the enormity of the fact.

I laughed, and Charley asked me what I was laughing about.

"Honor," I said.

"What?" he asked.

"Honor. I was laughing about honor."

"Neil," Charley said, tossing the bent knives and forks aside, onto the ground, "I just purely don't understand you. Not a goddam thing."

"You're a good man, Charley."

"That may be," he said, "but I'll tell you this: If these goddam knives and forks don't stop getting bent, I'm going to have to hunt up a new dishwasher."

"And spoons," I said.

"Yes, goddamit, and spoons," he said.

When he went back in, I lighted a cigarette and tried to figure out what he was trying to accomplish by such threats.

Then I closed my eyes for a while, and when I opened

them, the girl with white hair was standing there on the cinders of the parking lot.

And she said, "It doesn't make any difference. *I* will always think you're nice."

When she said that, I cried.

But there was no one around to notice, so it didn't make any difference.

Tonight, it rained again.

For the first time in my life, I was frightened by thunder.

What does it mean?

That's a question I ask too much.

I also make that kind of statement too often.

And that.

Etcetera.

I am going slowly but surely.

I can feel my self-control running down like the gears in a damaged clock.

I hunted through my pockets for a half dollar or at least a quarter to give to them.

But I didn't even have a dime.

Wanda bought us all a beer at four o'clock, before the dinner rush.

She is a giver, too. Therefore, blessed.

I bless you, Wanda.

Billie Sue, where are you?

She keeps her face down, again, and will not look at me. She is ashamed for me because I bend knives and forks and spoons, and leave them lying in the dirt behind the C. & J. Restaurant, where they shine like bent and discarded stars.

This afternoon, during the long idle stretch between the lunch and dinner rushes, Charley came back to the kitchen again, and suggested that we go out in back for a talk.

We made small talk, smoked cigarettes and drank a couple of beers from the Ingle Hollow as we stood out there with the garbage cans, and the cracked cement retaining wall, and the hill behind, choked with poison ivy, sumac, wild hickory, mountain cherry, and I don't know what kinds of trees.

The flies were circling above the cans, and everything was hot and peaceful and quiet.

Someone had thrown the bent silverware away.

I had promised myself that I wouldn't do it again. Too dangerous and dishonorable.

Charley said, "Neil, you were on that bridge, weren't you?"

When he said that, I closed my eyes and laughed so hard I almost fell over.

But when I stopped laughing Charley was still just standing there, drinking the last of his beer, and waiting for me.

"Well?" he said.

"That is the craziest idea I ever heard of," I said.

I realized right then I should have asked him, "What bridge?" but I couldn't think straight. It was like he had hit me on the head with a hammer.

"That still doesn't answer my question," he said.

"No," I said, opening my eyes and looking at the exact center of his forehead. "I wasn't ever on that bridge."

Charley just shook his head and flicked his cigarette ash off, and said, "I knew you were in trouble, somehow, and I began to think about when it was you come to us. It was right around New Year's, the best I can figure. And I don't know how long you'd been drunk. But you sure as hell were in bad shape."

I closed my eyes again and felt the sun burning on the skin of my face. I dropped my cigarette and took a deep breath.

"Look here," Charley said. "I ain't going to do nothing against you. Get that through your head. You're the best and most honest goddam dishwasher I ever had in the C. & J. And that's the *damn* truth!"

"Where's Harlan?" I said.

"Harlan? What in the hell has *he* got to do with anything?"

"I was just wondering," I said.

"Well, you owe him a lot, Neil. That's for sure. If he hadn't gotten you in hand that day, you probably wouldn't be here now."

"Wouldn't be where?"

"Wouldn't be *alive*, dammit!"

"He's on a crusade, isn't he?"

Charley took a breath and said, "Yes, I suppose he is."

Then he was quiet for a few seconds, before he said, "Lookee here, Neil. Is there any goddam reason you got to stand there with your eyes closed?"

I opened my eyes, and there in the distance the little white-haired girl was standing, looking at me.

"I ain't going to do a goddam thing," Charley said. "So for Christ's sake, calm down."

"I'm all right," I said.

"The way I figure it is you were in one of them cars that went down, and you bumped your head and got that amnesia people talk about. And you was wandering around down here, half out of your head from that bump and the drink both. Is that right?"

"That's pretty close," I said.

"Well, lookee here, Neil. If you want some help to find out who you are, or to get back to wherever you come from, I'll give you a hand. And if you don't want nobody to mess with you, that's okay with me too."

The little girl had gone away.

"Fine," I said. "And thanks."

I don't know whether I can sleep tonight, or not.

What's the matter with you, Billie Sue?

I'm going up to the old house and drink some of the wine I left up there.

I've been thinking that I left the old house too soon. I hadn't learned to love it yet. We have to learn to accept and even love the condition we find ourselves in. There's honor in this.

Should I have crossed the bridge?

I know it will be peaceful up there in the abandoned house, and maybe I can think.

I wish I could go back to the C. & J., and that it would be full of people, hurrying and laughing. And I could smell soap and hot water, and have stacks of dirty plates and saucers and cups and glasses and silverware. Which I could scrub and rinse clean, and return clean.

Clean. Clean. Clean.

Billie Sue, don't leave me. I could almost hear you talking to me today, and you were talking about leaving me.

There is something terribly wrong with that woman, but I love her anyway. Very much.

Clean and alive and warm and loving. These constitute honor in a woman.

I was drunk today and am still.

Somewhere, a filthy pale possum noses in garbage, looking for the gold in my teeth and the rings on my rotting fingers. I am a poisonous corpse, and I glow in the dark.

Liars abound and thrive, and the world is full of wickedness.

I am possessed by a demon, which keeps telling me I am free and rational.

But I am crazy. All the time. I should be put in an institution for the sake of all concerned.

Why don't people rise up against me? Why can't they understand the danger we are in?

I can almost smell something burning deep inside my mind.

Billie Sue was crying today.

Although I didn't see much, because I worked with my eyes closed most of the time.

Wanda came up and said, "Why don't you just make yourself blind, and be done with it?"

Charley didn't see a thing. And he didn't say anything, either.

Help me, Billie Sue!

Help me, help me, help me.

I love you, but you are slipping away.

As if a swift current is carrying you.

Your eyes are straight. It's the world that's crooked.

Monday.

It rained and stormed last night, but mostly the storm was only thunder and lightning.

This morning I decided to go to Harlan's trailer and retrieve the revolver.

After the breakfast rush, I walked down the street and crossed it by the Texaco station, where a gasoline truck was filling the pumps. Like some cumbersome female beast giving suck, its tubes screwed tight to the valves of the storage pumps, and waves of fumes wiggling like ghosts of gelatin in the air above.

Behind the station, however, the odor of the fumes was replaced by another odor —a deeper, more ancient, more offensive one.

I was sick from drinking, and this stink began to work at me, so that by the time I had gotten back to the trailer, I was almost ready to vomit.

There were flies circling the trailer, and the sunlight on the aluminum almost blinded me. I could even imagine that the numbers Harlan had painted were moving, edging forward and backward, like rolling beads of darkness in the blinding light.

The trailer looked tilted, only I might have been walking crooked.

The door was unlocked, and when I shoved it open, I heard the buzz of a thousand flies. The closeness and heat were terrible. Like a burning coffin.

Harlan's body lay peacefully on its back, with the legs crossed. The face was covered with a trembling, electric veil of flies, and the stink was profound, overwhelming, adamant and loathsome beyond description.

I took the revolver off the shelf, and left the trailer as fast as I could.

Up by the Texaco station, gasoline was still being fed into the underground storage tanks, and one of the attendants, Wendall Burgess, was filling a car with gas.

He yelled out at me, "Tell that old fucker to shit someplace else, will you? He's going to stink up the whole *town!*"

I walked about fifty yards up the street to a phone booth. I went inside, dug a dime out of my pocket, and phoned the sheriff's office.

I told them I *knew* it would happen. I could sense it, just looking at Harlan.

I didn't give them my name, but simply hung up and went back to the C. & J.

We are what we remember. And what we remember is circumscribed by what we cannot bear to remember. Or do not understand.

I went to the Ingle Hollow and had a couple of drinks.

Then I returned late to the C. & J., and Wanda asked me where I'd been.

"Harlan is on a crusade," I told her.

She just looked at me, and then walked away.

I gave the gun back to Charley.

Billie Sue was attending a funeral in another town, and Charley's sister was helping out.

All afternoon I kept imagining I could smell the trailer.

I went outside once, but the little girl with white hair was not there.

I had this dream. Or actually a fantasy, of sorts. It was while I was lying in bed half-asleep.

God was standing in His orchard, stunned by His own perfection. He was picking fruit from His most magnificent tree, and the fruit was delicious beyond understanding. I don't know what kind it was but each fruit was as full and warm as the breast of a young woman, and its juice was the secret of life, which even God, in His perfect wisdom, could only grope to understand.

But something deep inside all this perfection was wrong.

A breeze, smelling of green growth and salt, the element of life, stirred in God's hair and beard. And He muttered with vague uneasiness as He reached for the fruit and ate it, with unceasing hunger and undiminished satisfaction.

But something was wrong.

It was only upon looking down that He realized that His legs had sunk into the ground, and His arteries and veins had begun to take root in the earth.

Because we become what we love. Even God.

Let's say the earth was truth. Or the past.

God was honorable, and did not want to sacrifice the glory of love by becoming one with the object, so with infinite pain and travail He extricated each heavy foot from the hungry earth, and staggered away, drunk with loss.

Tears streamed down into His beard.

He walked until He imagined a river before Him. And being omnipotent, imagination was identical with creation; and the river appeared before Him. And then He thought of a bridge, and suddenly it rose higher than He had dreamed (or thought He had dreamed), and birds circled each lofty pillar of its supports, and God was pleased with what He saw.

So He crossed the bridge in the silence of His waiting Mind, which according to the same logic as that above, was identical to the tangible world which supported His feet as He walked.

But upon reaching the other side, He stepped into a void. Possibly His Mind had wandered. Maybe He was thinking of something else.

Whatever the reason, He found himself floating alone and free in a substance that was neither air nor water, but partaking of qualities of both.

He closed His eyes to think, and minutes, months, years passed by.

Until, out of a profound darkness of uncertainty, He saw the round globe of the earth come into view. And it was so lovely to Him, after eons of lonely drifting through nothing at all, that He fell in love with her.

For it was a woman, and silent, and alive, and warm.

And God fell upon the earth, moaning with love, and His sperm burst forth and made the stars and sun and moon out of this foam, and the earth filled with His seed and swelled and stuttered life from her flesh with trees and plants and grass and flowers and rivers and lakes and oceans and clouds and mankind.

This is all very strange. A strange kind of fantasy, and yet I believe there is meaning in it.

Beyond question.

Is it possible that even God, as fact or hypothesis (by implication) needs constantly to be reborn?

Yes, but we need a rock upon which to build.

Is the rock itself simply the quicksilver that animates our waking moments?

I must get back to work as soon as possible. Work is honorable and real.

You cannot question the cleanliness that emerges from my hands when I am washing dishes.

There's no need to.

Nothing is gratuitous.

Underneath all my confusions, I am exercising a deadly and relentless cunning.

What I am striving for is this: to emerge on the other side of the madnesses and confusions in which I find myself tangled and lost.

Actually, I have glimpsed this other side, and it is lovely and exalting beyond all words.

Sometimes I see it in the flash of an eye of the least likely—as with the hunchbacked pool player, or Mrs. Tarkington.

Someone you would never suspect. And most strangely, someone who would never suspect it of himself.

This afternoon I went to the Ingle Hollow for a drink. When I returned to the C. & J. I came in the back door, as usual. Then I went up to look through the swinging doors, and there he was.

He was talking to Charley, and lighting a pipe. Puffing strongly on it as he tamped the tobacco down.

As always, he looked very cool and calm.

Maybe he had traced so many missing persons down, and had worked on so many insurance-fraud cases, that he was bored by them.

Completely unruffled.

This was my impression.

Billie Sue was waiting on some men in the corner booth, and Wanda was serving ice water to a woman and her children in the third booth.

Charley was frowning and looking thoughtful, and saying something to him.

He was patient. You could tell he was simply waiting, because he knew it would all have to come out sooner or later.

You could tell he was on the side of an overwhelming statistical probability.

You could tell he was thinking he would be able to lead me back to the other side of the mirror, any time he wanted. But there's a mirror on the other side, too, that leads to a still deeper room.

Ridiculous metaphor!

I am not a male Alice. I'm not even the Mad Hatter. Although I am beyond any doubt psychotic.

I knew by the way his head was tilted that he was about to turn around and look at me, so I dodged out of the way, and along past Mrs. Tarkington, and out the back door.

My heart was thumping so fast I kept swallowing and taking deep breaths to stay alive as I worked my way along the back retaining wall toward my room.

In my room, I collected all the writing pads I had written in, Harlan's Bible, and a few extra clothes. I stuffed them all in the cheap valise I had bought at Mrs. Gain's Junk Store a few months back.

Then I made my way up the hillside, and in the direction of the old house.

This is where I am now.

Harlan is dead.

Billie Sue has left me.

Forever, forever. Forever.

I can't remember anything.

I am going to get drunk now, while it is still light.

There is only one regret: that I can't slip back, somehow, and leave a little gift for all of them.

But I guess I don't have anything to give. Only sixty-four cents and several bottles of wine. And this old house, filled with dust and dry air.

I want to tell it all before it's too late.

Who are you? Who is reading this?

Is it you, Billie Sue?

Yes, it is.

And the man named Reynolds. He will want to read it, too.

I won't take it with me.

Miss Temple, are you reading it? You didn't dream your advice would come to this, did you?

It frightens me, in going over my latest entry, to realize that it was almost the *last* one. It came close to being the very last entry, and there is a great deal to say.

For example, do you realize that *this is exactly like the last time*?

When I close my eyes, I can feel the coldness of that day and feel the warm engine throb beneath my feet pressed against the floorboards.

And then this enormous explosion, and the third or fourth car ahead simply disappears and the pigeons are fluttering high above, their wings clapping like human hands, applauding the gratuitous spectacle down below, which may have happened for their benefit.

Yes, I can see it clearly.

Will it ever be known who was on that bridge?

This is another step beyond the looking glass, and I am full of strength and courage, ready—even at this time—to step into a still deeper room.

All rooms have mirrors. All *things* have mirrors.

Yes.

These are not rooms of madness. No one admires rationality more than I do, and I have explained in this diary why this is so. Rationality and honor, these are the patrician virtues I love.

And generosity.

I'll take this idea with me, for it is indispensable to honor.

Yes, exactly like the last time.

Isn't it clear that I'm crossing another bridge?

Even though I love them all.

Especially you, Billie Sue, my bed, my bride, my bitch, my rocking boat!

Are you reading this, Billie Sue? If so, you hear my whispering. Because reading silently is a kind of whispering, isn't it?

Have I said that before?

The extent to which one understands his imprisonment is a measure of his freedom.

But the paradox is too glib, too easy. It is only a partial truth.

We take on new imprisonments when we despair of understanding the old. Yes. That's nearer to being true. That is a useful idea.

Unquestionably, I have a great deal to give to others, and my central problem right now, as I see it, is to release this strength in meaningful ways.

But what I am leaving behind! God, the enormity of it!

I can see them all: Wanda, Charley, Mrs. Tarkington, the hunchbacked pool hustler, the girl with white hair, the naked man and woman in this very house.

And Harlan, who is no more dead than these others whom I am leaving behind.

Question: How can you be reborn without killing others along with yourself?

Harlan, there were words we should have said to each other and things we should have heard from each other.

This is the tragedy.

You were an ignorant man, Harlan. But every breath you drew was deep and powerful.

And Billie Sue, who might even carry my seed deep under her stomach. Who knows?

They are all ghosts. And so are you.

And so am I.

But there is no turning back.

You step off the bridge, and it evaporates, it crumbles behind you. For what you had just stepped on was in the past, and the past no longer exists. Therefore, the bridge has always just collapsed. And all those you left behind are caught in limbo, voiceless and forgotten.

Harlan, we are all demons and crusaders, changing roles every minute, and lost in a jungle of cross-purposes.

And someone else, too, for a word of parting.

Yourself. You who are reading this.

Do you hear me whispering, and can you understand?

I know a great deal about you, because you have heard my voice.

You are there, and I feel your breath on this paper.

I give you my blessing, because who knows when he suddenly becomes sacred?

I am leaving tonight.

I will be drunk again on cheap wine, and I will go walking off under the trees, up the steep mountainside, in the direction of the moon and the stars and the heavens.

Harlan is listening to me, and Billie Sue is weeping in her pillow. Harlan the Father, and Billie Sue, the holiness of spirit and love made flesh.

Before long, I will start another diary.

God help me, but it may turn out like this one!

Honor is courage. The night is more beautiful than anyone could imagine. Billie Sue is praying for me, and I don't have anything left to fear.